IN THE SAME BOAT

BY THE SAME AUTHOR

In the Same Boat

By
KITTY BARNE

Illustrated by
RUTH GERVIS

DODD, MEAD & COMPANY
NEW YORK   1945

COPYRIGHT, 1945
BY KITTY BARNE

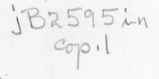

★   ★   ★   ★

PRINTED IN THE UNITED STATES OF AMERICA

Contents

Contents

Illustrations

IN THE SAME BOAT

SHIPWRECK

Chapter I

> 1 <

BRIDGET wriggled in her seat and the woman next to her with a little boy of two on her lap said, "Sit quiet, there's a dear. He's just getting off."

"Sorry," said Bridget, and tried to keep more still. You couldn't even wriggle without disturbing someone.

This was the third day in the lifeboat, of sitting cramped up on a bench-like seat, and she wasn't used to it yet, not nearly. If only my mind would sit still my body would, she said to herself; but nothing would stop her mind playing round the subject of Antosia. How was she? Where was she? Which of the other boats was she in?

They'd had different boat stations; that was the trouble. When they'd made friends, a thing they'd done straight off, almost as soon as they'd gone aboard, they had tried to get that changed; but the purser, who had seemed as good a person to ask as any, had only told them to run away and play. If ever they had occasion to *use* the boat stations, he told them, they would have no time to notice

who was there and who wasn't, they'd be so busy saving
their own skins. But he was quite wrong. They had used
them and it did matter. It mattered more than anything
in the world that Antosia was in one of those other boats
that dotted the glittering water like black fish with one
fin showing, instead of being squashed up on this seat,
taking her turn at holding Mrs. James's Boysie.

"Glare, isn't there?" said Mrs. James. "Don't you go
staring over the water like that or you'll get a headache.
Like to stand up? I never could keep still more than a
minute when I was eleven."

Bridget stood up and stretched out her arms above her
head. She was twelve, as a matter of fact, but that didn't
seem to make the sitting still any easier. What she wanted
was wings—wings to fly up into the glimmering sky; then
if Antosia had wings, too—and if anyone had them, Tossie
would—she'd rise up out of her boat and away they'd go,
sailing into the blue like larks, with Tossie singing for them
both . . .

"I don't like this boat," said Bobby White in his wail-
ing voice for the hundredth time. Even if you're only six,
you oughtn't to go on and on like that.

Bridget sat down again and asked "Why?" rather
sharply.

"Becos . . . becos . . ."—Bobby disliked it for such
dozens of reasons that he could hardly pick out a special
one—"it's got no proper deck to play on."

The sailor at the tiller gave a wintry gleam of a grin
at that. He was a youngish man with the sailor's searching,
faraway look in his eye. Nobody was talking much, but
Bridget thought she might as well venture a question.

"D'you think we'll ever know who's in those other boats?"

"Sure to. One of these days."

"Could we ask?"

"'Course you can ask."

"Soon?"

"Soon as we land."

What was the good of that? It was three days since the torpedo had hit them and their ship had disappe̶̶̶d, an enormous hotel of a ship, a little town almost, gone—in twenty minutes, swallowed up by the sea. For three days Antosia had been in a boat like this, hating it because, unlike most people, she hated the sea. Bridget had never been able to make her lean over the taffrail and look down on that lovely green-purple, ice-blue and silver world that made you think of mermaids, or go to the stern to watch the highroad of foamy wake they left behind. Antosia kept as far "inland," as she called it, as she could, close to the cabins. She turned her back on the dipping, rolling horizon that rose and fell in a way Bridget found entrancing and thought hard about horses and forests.

"But if you love horses so much, you ought to feel as if you were riding," Bridget had argued, trying to win her over. "We *are* riding, riding the waves—skimming along the top of them. Think of a sea gull—"

"I won't. I'll think of a hen."

"But it's glorious—the sea's glorious—"

"Not for me. It's different for you. You live on an island"—Antosia spoke beautiful English with a clipped, over-distinct, foreign accent—"a small island. If I lived on a small island, I should always be afraid I was going to fall off it into the sea—the disgusting sea. In Poland we drive miles and miles, on and on and on, through forests of trees. The road is like a tunnel through green, green, green—it never stops, it never could stop, it goes on till it gets to Russia and even then it goes on, further and further. You couldn't have a road like that in England."

No, you couldn't. Antosia, Bridget thought, came from Poland, and Poland was quite different from England, just as Poles were quite different from English people. It was just that difference that made having a Polish friend the exciting thing it was. She and Tossie didn't like the same things either to eat, or drink, or wear, or to do; they disagreed about nearly everything they discussed. Bridget learned once and for all what arguing can be when you're both perfectly sure you are right—yet they were friends.

"You'll find a girl about your own age on board," her father had said. "She's a Pole, Antosia Boryna. I've just met her father who's here buying and selling horses—a fascinating chap. I never heard anyone tell a better story. He had an English mother, I believe, anyway he speaks English perfectly. You might look out for this girl." So Bridget had looked out for her, and, as happens sometimes, they made friends at the first glance.

And now here they were, not even in the same boat.

She gave a sigh that was almost a groan.

"Hungry, are you?" inquired Bobby's mother kindly.

"No, thank you. Not really." She had been hungry the first day because the captain had decreed that, as they'd had good meals the day before, they should skip a day's food and have nothing but their water ration. (The captain happened to be in their boat, a great bit of luck, Bridget thought; and another reason why she longed to have Antosia beside her.) Mrs. White was a friendly, understanding sort of person, even if she did let Bobby whine, so Bridget went on to explain the sigh: "It's just that I've a friend in one of the other boats."

"I see. D'you know which one?"

"I think it's Number Four but I'm not sure. Anyhow, I don't know which Number Four is."

"We could find that out. We're all going to meet up again tonight, the captain says, as soon as it's getting dark. We'll ask, shall we? Who is the friend?"

"Antosia Boryna."

"What, that fascinating little Polish thing?"

"Yes. Her father's fascinating, too, Daddy said so. She's my best friend, and I keep on wondering about her."

"Well, I expect she's all right. About the same as we are, anyway."

"But she hates the sea. She simply loathes it."

Mrs. White made a face and said they were none of them too keen on it at the moment.

"Yes, but she hates it anyhow, whether she's been torpedoed or not. She must be miserable in a boat like this, with it all so close."

"Poor child. We'll find out which Number Four is and then you can keep an eye on it. Now why not put your head down on my lap and have a sleep till the time comes to ask. Move up, Bobby."

➤ 2 ◄

By the time Bridget woke up the sun was sliding down the sky and the scattered boats were making their way towards the captain's. She sat up and gave Mrs. White a gentle prod.

"All right, I haven't forgotten," and she called out, "Could you tell us which is Number Four, please?"

It turned out to be the big one in charge of the First Officer. He apparently had something to say and brought his boat up very close.

"D'you want me to ask about that child?" murmured Mrs. White, but before Bridget had time to do more than nod her head she heard something that drove every word away. She couldn't believe her ears. No, she *couldn't*.

"Got anyone of the name of Bridget Heath, sir?" the First Officer was shouting against the breeze.

Had they! Just *had* they!

"Yes. Me," piped up Bridget in a thin squeak of a voice that no one heard.

"Yes," cried Mrs. White, rather louder.

"Here, sir," sang out the sailor at the tiller. "Kiddy alongside here."

"Yes, we have," shouted the captain. "One of the children."

"Well, one of my children, a girl, wants to join up with her." The First Officer sounded quite fatherly. "She can't seem to settle without her. Will you allow it, sir?"

"Take her in, d'you mean?"

"That's what she wants. Polish child, Ann—what's your name, tell me again. How d'you spell it?"

And out came Antosia's clear, high voice over the water —she could talk more distinctly than anyone on earth when she liked, or so Bridget thought—"Antosia Boryna."

"Relation?" inquired the captain, who never did anything in a hurry.

"No. Friend," called Antosia.

"Pass, friend, and all's well," said someone, trying to be funny.

"Right. We'll take her," agreed the captain. "Send along a blanket with her, will you? We're a bit short."

And in another minute Antosia was hoisted in, blanket and all, and handed down across the thwarts until she reached her place between Mrs. White and Bridget.

"Hallo, Tossie," said Bridget because she couldn't think of anything better to say.

Antosia was half laughing, half crying, her wavy brown hair falling in a curtain over her face as it always did. "Oh, I thought I should never see you again!" she cried, the tears streaming down, and she seized Bridget's sleeve and kissed it—that was what the people did at home in Poland when they wanted to give you a special greeting, she'd told her English friend. Oh, well, it wouldn't have been Tossie if she'd just grinned back and said, "Hallo." Tossie was different.

➤ 3 ◄

The extra blanket was a great blessing. It helped to keep the two girls warm at night and, propped up by the end of a broken oar when the wind allowed, it made them a tent by day into which they could retire and listen to Antosia's stories. It was a magic cave, Bridget decided, because in it they traveled so far from the boat, so far from the extraordinary fact that they'd been torpedoed and shipwrecked like people in the newspapers, and that land was miles and miles away and there didn't seem to be any ships about to pick them up.

"It's hot," Antosia would say when the wind dropped and the sail was no good and the sailors were forcing them-

It made them a tent by day

selves to row, three men to the great heavy oars. "Let's go home and see if the winter has come." And she'd tell about the lovely Polish snow that was frosty and powdery so that it wouldn't make snowballs, that shook off your coat even when you fell into a snowdrift, leaving you dry as a bone, and how when it came the farmers took the wheels off their carts and put on wooden runners, turning them into sleighs.

"Sleighs!" The very sound of the word was cool and swift and beautiful. "Bells?" Bridget asked.

"Yes, bells all over the harness and the sun like diamonds and the blue houses with snow roofs—"

"Not *blue*?"

"Yes, the little houses, cottages. And that sort of sleigh is difficult to keep straight—it slips and slides and goes sideways and everyone falls out." Tossie's laugh was rather like bells itself, Bridget thought. "But no one is ever hurt because our snow is so soft and dry. My father had a beautiful sleigh with iron runners—with two horses we flew along. And one day they went into a snowdrift, a big one like a hill, and they pulled them out with cows. My father said it was a deep disgrace for his horses that they should have been saved by *cows*."

"Can you eat it, your snow?" Bobby White, who generally came into the cave too, always brought the conversation around to food.

"Yes."

"What's it like?"

"Cool."

"Lemony?"

"Not exactly. More cucumber."

It did them good to think of that delicious cold snow when the water ration seemed a long way off. Inside that tent they tumbled in and out of snowdrifts and watched the snowploughs making a way for the trains and smoothing the roads for traffic; a surface of brown snow rather like sand was good for horses, Antosia said.

"Brown snow? Like chocolate?" asked Bobby.

"More like cocoa."

And after that they fell silent, thinking about cocoa, mugs of cocoa and sugar in a bowl so that you helped yourself, and biscuits out of a huge tin.

The days went on, slipping into each other, driving towards them and streaming away behind them like the endless seas. There was a day of storm when the blanket was wrapped around both of the girls and Bobby, and the water came up nearly to their knees. There was one of complete calm, roastingly hot, when the sail flapped, use-less, and they lay rocking in the swell, drifting off their course until the men took to the oars again, exhausted though they were. There was a rain squall that soaked them to the skin, but it gave them a wash and filled up the pemmican tins they used for water and when the sun came out hotter than ever the boat steamed like a laundry and inspired Mrs. White to wash some clothes over the side. And there were other days of steady wind when their boat slipped along with the water gurgling and chuckling and slapping along her sides—a happy sound to Bridget, who loved boats and all their ways.

But Antosia only shivered and stopped her ears.

"I hate that water noise. It's the sea and it *gobbles*."

"It only gobbles under the floor boards. They'll be bail-ing again soon."

"It sucks at you, the sea does—sucks and sucks and gulps you down."

"It doesn't. It buoys you up. It's in a good temper now, slapping our boat along nicely."

"I don't like it. Let's talk about houses—houses and beetroot soup and pickled cucumber which you think you don't like, but that's because you don't know—"

And so it went on, night into day, day into night. The boatload grew more and more silent.

Antosia stopped her stories, even in the cave, because talking made her too thirsty. "Let's think of so-and-so by ourselves," she would say, and leave Bridget and Bobby to paint their own pictures with all the colors she had given them; the snow with its lavender-blue and purple shadows, the blue houses that winter thatched with white, the great trees with branches bending under the weight of the powdery stuff you could eat—yes, with a spoon and pretend it was sugar if you liked . . . and in five minutes they would be asleep.

Half the time they were asleep. The sun burnt them a darker and darker brown. Bobby White changed from a chubby little pink and white boy into a gnome; he was like the special Polish gnomes who go in for frightening horses, Antosia said. Boysie lay so still he was no trouble at all.

What was happening to all the people in the rest of the boats behind them they never knew nor cared. By the time they came to be picked up after nineteen days they were hardly aware of what was happening. Even Bridget, who was tough, had to be lifted out of her seat and hauled up the ladder, her legs seemed to have turned into paper.

And Antosia was worse. But she kept her wits about her. The moment she was on board she managed to produce a sentence in her clearest and most polite voice: "Please be sure this time that I have the same boat station as Bridget. She's my friend." Then she fainted.

> 4 <

Bridget was on her way home to Grannie and school. Her father was in the Indian Civil Service and her mother and three little brothers, the youngest of them Boysie's age, stayed in India with him—naturally.

"And of course there's no reason why you shouldn't, too, darling," her mother had said.

But Bridget would have none of that. It had always been arranged that she was to go to Ramparts School where her mother and her grandmother had gone before her. Twelve was the age to go, the Lower Fourth was the form to get into (and she only hoped she'd achieve it), and the September term was the one to begin at. She liked the sound of that school, she always had, and she was quite clear that, war or no war, she wanted to go to it.

Her parents in their hearts agreed with her.

"Very well, darling. In that case Daddy and I both think you'd better go now, while the going's fairly good, especially as it's such a bit of luck that if the school had to be turned out of its buildings, it should have gone so near Grannie. You'll be able to live with her and go as a day-girl. So nice for you."

But after all, the going hadn't been even fairly good and here she was in the ship that had rescued them, a long way off England and Grannie, and still further from the Lower Fourth because all the knowledge she'd ever acquired in the way of lessons was oozing out of her. Had oozed. She had already forgotten pretty well everything she knew except how to read.

And Antosia, when she tried to explain, didn't understand a bit.

"What does it matter?"

"I shall be so late. We're not going to get to England for ages—cargo to discharge or something."

"Late? Who minds being late for school?"

"I do. Mummy says you stay in a form for a year and then you all go up together. You go up to a new room and a new mistress and a new desk and new work and it's simply frightful to be left behind."

Antosia gave her a puzzled stare.

"Is it then a race, your school?"

"No, not exactly. You have to keep up though. Mummy

was rather good. She was never left behind once; nor was Grannie."

"A party of you, is it? A bunch? But your bunch will never leave you behind, Bridget. You'll run and catch them up. You're what my father calls a stayer."

"What's that mean?"

"It's a good thing to be. He likes it in a horse."

"Yes, but what does it *mean?*"

"I don't think I know. Perhaps an 'active.' "

"And what does an 'active' mean?"

"The opposite to a 'passive,' I suppose."

That was no help either; it only reminded Bridget in a vague, unpleasant sort of way that once upon a time there had been things called French verbs. Tossie was having one of her "knowing" attacks when she said things no one understood.

Bridget frowned, and Antosia, who was quick to know what the other person was thinking, said, "Only words— words are nothing. I don't see what you are frowning at. It is all very simple. You will go to your English school. It is there for you. It is alive."

"Oh, yes, it's there all right. They've moved it into a huge great house near Grannie."

"Polish schools are all dead, I expect," said Antosia cheerfully. "But only for a time. They will come alive again. Everything in Poland comes alive again, nothing there dies forever."

"And then will you go to one?"

"My half-uncle will arrange," and she spread her hands in a way that finished the school conversation.

Now wasn't it like Antosia to have a half-uncle as her only relation in England.

"*Half*-uncle? But you can't have a half-*uncle*. Half-brother or half-sister, but no one has a half-uncle. You've got it wrong."

"Mine is a half," said Antosia with dignity. "My English grandmother died and after years my grandfather married again, a Polish lady this time, and he is her son. He is my father's half-brother and so he is my half-uncle."

There didn't seem to be anything more to be said about that.

"Do you know him?"

"I have never seen him. But they say he is like my father, so I shall like him."

"Will he come and meet you?"

"Of course he will."

"And where will you go?"

"I don't know. Somewhere with him."

Antosia was very calm about her future plans, thought Bridget. She herself, though she had no qualms about her school—she felt half there already, she had heard so much about it—had terrible qualms about living with Grannie. She hadn't seen her since she was five. Sweets in a drawer and tunes to dance to were all she could remember, not much to go upon when you're going to live with a person. Still, a great deal more than Tossie had.

"Does he do anything, your half-uncle? I mean is he a doctor or lawyer or anything?"

Antosia opened her blue eyes wide in an amazed stare.

"Do anything? But he will of course be fighting for Poland."

"But how can he meet you if he's doing that?"

She shrugged her shoulders.

"At present it is in England that he fights for Poland.

He escaped. One day it will be in Poland herself, my father says. But not soon. No, not soon."

Once again she finished off the conversation. You only had to mention Poland and Tossie became completely grown up and as far away as the stars. All Bridget knew of soldier relations—and she had a good many—was that they were quite the last people who could set up a home for you. However, "stayer" that she was, she pursued the subject.

"You can't possibly go living with your half-uncle if he's in the Army. I'm perfectly certain about that. I wish you'd make him send you to my school. Why couldn't you?"

Antosia looked thoughtful; but not, Bridget decided, displeased at the idea.

"Would you like to have me at your school?"

"I should love it. It'd be just perfect—" Somehow Tossie should be placed in the Lower Fourth, too. She spoke three languages besides her own, English perfectly, French pretty well, German quite enough. She didn't know much of anything else except the history of her own country, with which she was filled to the brim—but Ramparts would see to that. "Oh, do make him!"

Antosia gave a laugh; and then tossed her head like a proud pony.

"But I am Polish. I shall be in the Polish Army like my uncle—half-uncle."

"But you can't. Not yet. You're not thirteen till next Tuesday."

"Tuesday, Tuesday, Tuesday—" Tossie jumped up and danced around the little bit of deck they were allowed to use, throwing her arms up in the air, stamping her feet,

making her own music by singing at the top of her voice.
"Come on, Bridget. Dance with me. I'll show you."

But Bridget shook her head. She knew no amount of
showing would make her dance like that; nothing would
make her, not even a birthday next Tuesday, with the
whole ship preparing a birthday party. Tossie had nearly
died for three days after they had been rescued, then she
had picked up quicker than any of them. Her eyes were
still a size too large and her legs and arms still like match
sticks, but life had come rushing back to her like a tide
with the wind behind it, and they felt she did them all
great credit. With her dancing and singing and playing
about she was something worth rescuing. No wonder the
cook was making her a cake with thirteen dates sticking
up around it instead of candles and a little mound of
sugar in the middle with a paper flag in the Polish colors
to crown it.

Tossie stopped as suddenly as she had begun and flung
herself into a deck chair.

"My legs are trembling and shaking like an old, old,
broken-winded mare. I'm dead. I can't dance. I never shall
dance again."

"Why don't you do a little at a time, like Mrs. White
said? Of course you're dead."

"Grandmother Bridget," murmured Antosia, with her
eyes shut, "your school is a school for English grandmothers." And before Bridget had time to find an answer
to that she was asleep.

"Mum says she's like a young cat." Bobby White, still
rather a gnome, appeared. He came after the two girls
when he could, hoping that the days of the blanket tent
might come back and let him hear some more of Antosia's

"Come on, Bridget. Dance with me"

stories. "Not a kitten, she says, but a young cat. D'you think she'll get up and dance again?"

"No."

"Nor sing or anything?"

"No."

"Oh." Bobby was disappointed but resigned. "Then perhaps you'd better read to me."

He produced a book with a picture of a ship in full sail on the outside. If he couldn't have the spoken word, print was better than nothing. But the cover was a fraud; there were no more pictures inside, only maps with arrows showing the way the winds blew and the tides flowed and the currents ran. It was very dull and soon they both joined Antosia in slumber.

"Isn't it wonderful the way the children are sleeping it off," said Mrs. White to Mrs. James when she found them.

> 5 <

But everything comes to an end in time, even a long voyage. The moment arrived when the magic word "*Land!*" tore round the ship like a little live animal. It was in the early morning and Bridget at once dragged Antosia out of bed.

"Come on, Tossie, wake up! Stick on a coat and come on deck."

"Why? What's the matter? What are you so excited about?"

She rubbed the sleep out of her eyes to stare at such an unusual Bridget.

"Land! England!"

"Your country!"

It was as if a bell rang inside Tossie. Here was something in Bridget she really could understand. She sprang up at once, slipped on the fur boots someone had *lent* her, and for the first time allowed herself to be drawn to the rail, to lean her arms on it and stare over the water, as all the English people aboard were doing.

"Where is it?"

The seas below were a dull, heaving green-gray, with a white cap here and there; the sky was the same gray, without the shine. They seemed to be inside a gray ball.

"Over there, see." Bridget stretched out one of Tossie's arms and looked down it as if down a telescope. Where the grays met and merged a smudge showed, a darker gray still. You couldn't say England looked an exciting place exactly, Bridget had to admit; still, there it was—England!

"You love it?" questioned Antosia, trying to gaze enthusiastically at the smudge.

"Oh, er, yes . . . rather . . ." said Bridget. No one ever said so, of course. "There'll always be one."

"One what?"

"There'll always be an England. That's a song, you know."

"*An* England?" Antosia frowned—she always puzzled about such queer, unnecessary things, Bridget thought. "An England, somewhere—it doesn't matter where? Is that what it means?"

"No, not a bit. It means something quite different. It means—" but Bridget got no further.

"I would never say *a* Poland. I would say *my* Poland. There'll always be my Poland." And Antosia stared broodingly into the gray.

"Well, anyhow, that's England, and that's where your half-uncle will be meeting you. The captain says we'll get in tonight and I shouldn't wonder if he and my Grannie weren't just starting off in the same train. I hope they are, I hope they're in the same carriage, making terrific friends."

"England!" cried Antosia in a sudden joyful yell and made one of her quick changes of mood, seizing Bridget round the waist with one arm, flinging up the other, stamping and skipping down the deck with her.

"That's the stuff. Say it with the feet, let the little tootsies have the word," called a sailor, grinning. "No place like 'ome after all." And he'd have joined in if just then an officer hadn't appeared.

The two girls hung over the rail most of the day while England loomed darker and larger out of the mist. Anyone would know it was an island, Antosia said, it looked so at home in the water. Like a duck swimming in a pond. She liked the surf, too. England wore an opossum coat rimmed with ermine. She was, in fact, liking it more and more, to Bridget's great pleasure, when something happened—a warning of some kind—and instead of going on, they had to spend the night "somewhere else," as the Second Officer put it.

Antosia went into a transport of rage at the delay—"To be so close and then to turn away, how can you *bear* it?"

But, Bridget explained, no one ever fussed over things at sea. It was like fussing over the weather, it did no good at all; much better to go to bed and perhaps it would be a finer day tomorrow.

So to bed they went and, lo and behold, it *was* a finer day. The wind had dropped, the sun was out, the sky was blue, the water was all diamonds and sapphires. There was no gray anywhere. Though it was November, it might have been May.

"There! You see," said Bridget. "That wait was a very good thing as it turned out."

"But does your weather often change its mind like this— be hateful, be beautiful, be winter, be summer?" asked Antosia, now finding everything amazing and exquisite.

"Often. All the time. You never know. But this is a bit of luck. It's far better for you to see England and your half-uncle for the first time on a fine day." Bridget was as pleased and proud as if her country had done it entirely to welcome Tossie.

There was no packing to be done. The clothes they wore had been washed and ironed for them during the first week aboard the rescue ship, which they had spent in their bunks, and they had no others, no luggage at all except Antosia's blanket, which she held proudly over her arm. They ate their last breakfast, and said some of the good- byes, then went on deck to spend the rest of the time hanging over the rail. Antosia might still say she hated the sea and hoped never to see it again, but the fascination of watching England emerge from it was too much for her.

"It's no good your saying you're never going on board a ship again," declared Bridget. "You'll have to."

"Never, never, never."

"But we're an island. Boats belong to us; they're like your sleighs."

"I shall fly. I flew to India with my father. I shall fly to Poland. Your island is very wet. It glistens with wet."

Mrs. White was beside them now, hoisting up Bobby to look at the quay where groups of people were clustered. "Can you see Daddy? Look, that tall man in the bowler hat. No, not the soldier, further along."

"Can you see your half-uncle?" whispered Bridget.

No, Antosia couldn't. She didn't know him by sight, but there was no one there who looked in the least like an uncle. One or two people might be Bridget's Grannie. The two girls stared at them all, trying to decide which it might be.

"Better wait till we get a bit closer and we can see faces. Grannie never used to have a hat on and all these people have got hats. I suppose if your half-uncle's so like your father, you'll recognize him."

"Oh, yes, and he'll recognize me. We'll both say, 'That's a Pole.' "

Antosia was very cheerful. Bridget, who was yawning all the time, feeling very blue, hating the idea of leaving this ship which had become home after the long time on board her, hating still more the idea of exchanging Tossie for a Grannie she hardly knew, thought her very brave.

"I don't believe he'll say that about you. You look just the same as the rest of us. It's inside you're different—" then the hard fact struck her and gave her a shock, as hard facts do. Here was Tossie going off with this uncle and she herself with Grannie. What was going to happen to their friendship? What? "Tossie, when shall we see each other again?"

"Oh, soon. Quite soon," said Tossie comfortably.

"How d'you know it'll be soon?"

"We're friends."

"Yes, but we ought to make plans, make your uncle— half-uncle—make plans."

"If he is like my father, he will be bad at plans. But I shall do it."

"How?"

"I made them put me into your boat, didn't I? And at first the First Officer said, 'Don't be silly,' and a lady beside me said, 'You're old enough to know better.' I told her I did know better—that was just it. And I told the officer I should come to you or die. And I came, didn't I?"

"Yes, you did, but that's not at all the same. We ought to make a plan—" but as she had no plan ready, Bridget produced a sixpence which the Second Officer had kindly cut into two neat half-moons for her.

"You take this, Tossie."

"What is it?"

"It means we're two halves making one. Now don't go losing it or giving it away or anything. It's money, but you can't buy anything with it without its half. See?"

"I see. Is that an English custom, to break it in half?"

"I don't know that it's particularly English but I had that sixpence in the boat and the Second Officer said it would be quite a good thing to do as it must be a pretty lucky sixpence—I was telling him about you. He's got a lucky sixpence himself, a sort of keepsake someone gave him. You keep it for somebody else's sake. That's the idea."

"It means we're two friends, does it?"

"Yes. And, look here, I've written my address down on this post card. He gave it to me, with the stamp and all—"

"Green Hedges, what does that mean?"

"It's the name of the house. You have hedges round houses in the country and Grannie's are green, I suppose. Now you're to send me your address the moment you know it. Promise."

"Great-grandmother Bridget," murmured Antosia. But she put the card safely away in her pocket, beside her other

possession, the comb one of the sailors had given her, and
promised. By the time she had done that they were a good
deal closer to the dockside and a tug was pulling their
bows around to let them lie alongside properly.

"I think that might be Grannie in the sort of greeny-
gray clothes," said Bridget.

"But won't she have white hair?"

"Oh, yes, I suppose she will. Well, then, perhaps it's
the old lady with the stick. Or what about that one waving
the handkerchief? Oh, Tossie, look at that angel of a
cairn!"

"What's a cairn?"

"A sort of dog. Look at him, lugging along that great
tall woman. She's late, or he thinks she is. Oh, isn't he
a darling?"

But Antosia didn't think him a darling. A small dog that
stood on his hind legs, held up by his leash, yapping his
head off, wasn't the sort of dog she liked at all. And there

"Or what about that one waving the handkerchief?"

was Bridget with eyes for nothing else.

"Perhaps you'd rather have a dog to meet you—" she began sarcastically. But Bridget missed the sarcasm completely and only said she would, much rather, she'd like nothing better, but that there'd be no such luck.

"Perhaps the owner is your grandmother." Antosia found nothing impossible.

"Not a hope. Just look at her. Quite wild—nice and wild, I mean, with her hair blowing about and those huge gloves, but she doesn't look as if she was meeting anybody. And anyone could see she's not a Grannie. It's the green-gray one, I'm sure it is. Sort of sure and solid and slow, like grandmothers are. D'you see your uncle?"

"Half-uncle."

"Half-uncle then. What's his name? You never told me."

"He's always called Krak after Krak of Krarkov. That was the Hooded Knight who killed the Dragon."

"I know. We've a knight like that, too. Ours is George."

"Uncle Krak, I shall call him."

"Then I'd better call him Uncle George—it's a sort of translation." A sensible English name, Bridget thought; it would surely belong to a nice, reasonable uncle with graying hair and perhaps a top hat, an uncle who would understand that she and Antosia must see a great deal of each other, meet every holidays at least, or, better still, go to the same school. "I feel as if I'd known Uncle George for years."

"But I don't see him."

"Nor do I."

There was no one even remotely resembling an Uncle George standing there on the quay. Bobby White's father was waving, the soldier with the plum-colored beret was waving and grinning from ear to ear, the woman with the cairn had picked him up and was waving his paw (so she was meeting someone after all)—yes, and the one who was probably Grannie was waving. The party of shipwrecked people, the boating party as Antosia called it, waved back, clustered together around the captain, and everyone cheered.

"Oh, it is *exciting*, arriving in England!" cried Antosia, her eyes shining; and she shouted a most un-English "*Huzzahola!* I must wave to someone—I shall wave to the soldier. Uncle Krak's late. My father is always late, too. You'd better wave to the dog, as you like him so much."

She didn't mind Uncle Krak being late; she seemed, in fact, to expect it. She cheered louder than anyone and waved frantically. The soldier, who was quite young, waved back, whether to Tossie or not, Bridget didn't know, both arms up, his bright beret twirling in one hand. Bridget thought she had never seen such waving, such a welcome.

Could he be a relation of Mrs. James? There she was beside them, with Boysie in her arms and joyful tears running down her face, she was so pleased to see someone. But he looked much too young to be Boysie's father—perhaps he was Mrs. James's brother, people do have very young brothers sometimes.

The ship drew closer and closer; the gangway, the little bridge that was to join them to England, appeared. The soldier crammed his beret on his head, took a flying leap and sprang up the gangway long before it was ready. "Antosia!" he cried, and poured out a flood of unintelligible language.

"Uncle Krak!" Tossie cried back, and he seized her in his arms and hugged her.

It was Uncle George. Now who but Antosia would have an uncle like that?

GREEN HEDGES

Chapter II

➤ 1 ◄

BRIDGET sat in the train, the puppy, James, asleep in her lap.

James had been almost as much of a surprise as Uncle George, and Grannie the greatest surprise of the lot.

The green-gray woman had come up the gangway and Bridget had stepped forward politely, feeling very shy, and said how d'you do?—and then if she didn't turn out to be the captain's wife.

"Richard!" she had cried and the captain, astoundingly, had kissed her. The old lady with two sticks was the doctor's mother; the one who had waved the handkerchief melted into the crowd and was lost. Everyone as she or he came up the gangway was claimed and swallowed up in hugs and handshakes. Antosia, arm and arm with her half-uncle, took no notice of anything. Bridget had stood there feeling more lonely than she ever had in her life.

Then a yapping, wriggling, hard little body was put into her arms, a cold, eager nose thrust itself under her chin, and someone said, "This is James, your dog, who's come to meet you. I remember even at five you had dog loves and journeys should end in lovers' meetings, so here he is." And lo! the tall, wild woman was Grannie.

She certainly was a most unexpected Grannie, in her tweed suit and long gloves, with her hat on the back of her head when everyone else wore theirs on their noses. She had talked to pretty well everyone on the ship and in two minutes she had known them better than Bridget had known them in a month. She wrung the captain by the hand and the green-gray woman too. She gave Bobby White a bar of chocolate, and admired Boysie James until you'd think there was no baby like him in the world. Bridget with James, a lump of pure inquisitiveness trying to put his nose into everything, followed Grannie around while she talked to every one of the shipwrecked passengers. She was thrilled by them all, and, even with their own greetings and welcomes, they seemed pleased to see her—but that, as Bridget was to find, was Grannie all over. People were her hobby, she loved them, and they seemed to know it.

Now she threw her hat off, took out a comb and tidied her hair at the glass in the railway carriage, talking all the time.

"I was so glad to see that plait of yours. Your mother had said, 'You'll know her by the plait,' and I did. We were so late this morning, James and I, no time for breakfast before we started. Then when we got there they said you weren't due for another half hour and we rushed off for a cup of coffee but before it was half down you were practically in and we had to rush back. James is as strong as a pony."

"Yes, Antosia and I were watching him pull you along."

"So clever of you to recognize me. And you seemed to recognize James, too—he thought so anyway. *What* an interesting lot of people, and *what* experiences to have all been through! Miracles, the lot of you. The only ones I didn't quite grasp was the child you were with and the young man in uniform you called Uncle George. *Is* he your uncle? No, he can't be—I saw 'Poland' on his sleeve."

Bridget explained and Grannie cried, "Oh, but how really thrilling—I wish I'd talked some more to him," and went on tidying herself until she began to look quite young.

"Could she come and see us later on—that girl, I mean?" It seemed to Bridget better to get it out at once. "She's my best friend."

"Is she? Was she in that boat with you?"

"Yes."

"Then of course she shall come. And the exciting uncle, too. Some day." Grannie's face clouded a little. "We shall have to fix it up with Mrs. Drake."

"Who's Mrs. Drake?"

"Well, Drake is really a farm laborer. They live close by and he and Mrs. Drake run Green Hedges for me in their odd moments. Very odd moments. You never know when they'll be there—it's just when they've nothing better to do, I think. You'll see. I haven't told her about James yet." A look that was almost guilty came over her face. She crammed on her hat without a further look at the glass and said, "You see, I can't cook. My generation never learned. They all do it now, all the young things, but we never did. So of course I'm thankful to have Mrs. Drake—*thankful*." But she sighed as if thankful was the last thing she felt.

"Antosia can cook."

Grannie shook her head.

"Children never can."

"She's very old in lots of ways—that comes of having traveled about with her father. She makes all sorts of funny Polish things, beetroot soup and something frightfully good they call Little Doves."

"Little Doves? They sound delicious. Well, of course that would make it easier, much easier. Now here we are— is my hat straight? Back to front? No, is it *really?* That better? Thank you, darling—I see you're going to be just the grandchild for me. Now here we are with London and an orgy of shopping before us. How nice to think that you haven't a stitch of anything in the world. We can start at the beginning and go on to the very end—shipwrecked mariner's privilege and consolation. I've got a list from Ramparts."

"Ramparts? Am I going to school at once?"

"Yes, as soon as we like. Now then, come along, let's enjoy ourselves. We'll begin with lunch."

➤ 2 ◄

Mrs. Drake opened the door; a dumpy figure like, Bridget thought, a halma man, with her white knob of a head and black body widening out into white again in her well-boiled, well-starched apron reaching down to her toes. "Cross," Bridget recognized, and vaguely wondered why: Grannie surely wasn't a person to be cross with.

However, there was no time to spend considering Mrs. Drake. The taxi was littered with clothes, hats, shoes, books. James had worried open some of the parcels, others

Mrs. Drake opened the door

had been tied up with string only and he could and did eat string by the yard. A bicycle whirled its wheels insecurely·on the roof, a hockey stick and two despatch cases fell out in the road the moment the door was opened.

An old, slow golden retriever came out, wagging his feathery tail, and picking up a shoe, carried it conscientiously into the house. "That's Rouge," said Grannie, introducing him. "He's a professional retriever, so he ought to be a help. There's the clever dog—now come back for something else, Rouge." (But Rouge didn't; he took the shoe and hid it under Grannie's bed, where it was lost for days.)

Grannie, her arms full of hats and books, reached her doorstep.

"Well, Mrs. Drake, er . . . here we are."

"So I see, madam."

There was something awful about that "madam." Mrs. Drake had once been first kitchen maid in what she called a "good" house and she never allowed it to be forgotten. There was nothing at all good, in her sense, about Green Hedges.

"It's nice someone has money to waste," she went on with a sniff (Bridget was to get to know those sniffs). "I shan't have to tell the lady when she calls for Savings."

"Oh, but you can't save on shipwrecked mariners whose clothes are all at the bottom of the sea." Grannie's smiling voice that had sent the people running in all the shops they went to, hurrying to find exactly the right things, eager to help such an unfortunate, took on the faintest note of exasperation.

"And what's this dog?"

"He's James. He's a new dog."

"Well, I'm not having him in my kitchen, so he needn't think it. Scat!" She flapped her apron at James, who at once seized a corner of it between his teeth. He bit into everything, out of fun, rage, curiosity, hunger, or just because teeth were there to be used. "Now look at him! Torn me apron, that's what he done. And calling him James like a footman. Never heard of such a thing."

"Like a footman, is it? It's so long since I've seen a footman—Bridget, get hold of him, darling. You must try to keep him in order. Very well, Mrs. Drake, we'll keep him out of your kitchen; of course we will."

But it wasn't Mrs. Drake's kitchen; she had one of her own in a cottage with a wonderful thatched roof only a quarter of a mile away—Grannie had pointed it out. Bridget would like to have said so but Grannie was continuing in the coaxing voice that Bridget was soon to know as the special one kept for Mrs. Drake. "Very good of you to have stayed so late. We've had no tea; we're simply starving. Is supper ready?"

"Yes." Mrs. Drake sounded a little mollified. "I got a nice little dinner for you, the pie's in the oven and the Queens pudding. And now if you've no further orders, madam, I'll be going back to Drake. He's had to get his own tea and what he'll say I don't know."

"I do," murmured Grannie as the door shut. "Nothing. Drake never says anything."

➤ 3 ◄

Further orders indeed! What orders there were at Green Hedges were given by Mrs. Drake herself, as Bridget was soon to find out. She didn't see much of her; in no time at all she was caught up in a routine that took her out of the house before that sour face appeared and returned her after it had left to attend to Drake's tea.

At eight o'clock Bridget kissed James good-bye and set off for Ramparts on her bicycle. Breakfast, prepared by Grannie, was supposed to be at half past seven, but was generally ready at ten minutes to eight and so eaten in a tremendous scurry. After she had gone, Grannie washed up in an even greater scurry, for fear Mrs. Drake should "look in" early for half an hour and find the remains of it on the table.

"But what would it matter if she does?" Bridget had very naturally inquired, and got a mysterious, "Oh, it would never do," in return. The truth was Mrs. Drake liked Grannie to be the kitchen maid she had once been herself, the hard-worked, lowly person who prepared the way for the cook. A cook in a good house should sail grandly in, all dressed in white like a surgeon, at ten o'clock, and if she hadn't gone and married Drake, that's the kind of cook Mrs. Drake would have been. This was the nearest she could get to it.

But once Bridget was at Ramparts, Green Hedges and all its affairs faded away into a vague haze. Everything at Ramparts was so definite, so certain, so incessant. There was something very satisfactory about the confident way it went on. You fitted into your precise place—as soon as you had a place—and then round you went with the whole vast wheel of it; there it was, revolving day by day, you with it, like the earth on its axis. From the moment you wheeled your bicycle in and stood it in exactly the right place, left your coat on the right peg and your shoes in the right pigeonhole, you knew what was before you—at nine, at quarter to ten, at half past ten, at Break, and so on throughout the day.

"You love it, don't you?" Grannie said, hearing about it all. "I did, too. You feel like part of the solar system, don't you, obeying enormous natural laws that have been there forever?"

But at first you were not a citizen of this fascinating world; you were a mere hanger-on. Not until you were part of a form did you really become an inhabitant, and for some days Bridget was not in a form. She did an examination paper very badly now and again, and was very kindly, if inquisitively, treated by everyone high and low because of the torpedo.

Was it so awful in the boat? Had she really been *starv-*

ingly hungry? What had happened to all the other people? Had she *seen* the torpedo? It was growing harder and harder to answer such questions. Those nineteen days of the boat were becoming more and more of a dream; the water sucking and chuckling under the footboards, the sting of the surf on her face that stormy day, the feel and taste of Antosia's snow when she fell into snowdrifts like sugar hillocks and cows came to pull her out—all these things faded in and out of each other until Bridget hardly knew which belonged to the boat and which to the tent of Antosia's blanket.

Only Antosia herself remained perfectly distinct—"my Polish friend." Bridget talked about her by the hour to anyone who'd listen. The other new girls were no longer new, the term was so far advanced, and she had no companion to share the perplexities of the great, strange place, to help her to ferret out such things as whether that was a Sixth Form girl or the games mistress who had spoken to her just now; whether you were supposed to go up certain senior stairs or not; whether you were to put down your name for hockey, if you wanted to play hockey or not.

"I'm not in a form yet, you see, Grannie. Only the seniors play hockey and I don't know if I am senior," Bridget explained when she arrived home, her brows knit with anxiety. "The Lower Fourth's senior—but I'm so *late.*"

"They're letting you down easy, that's all; allowing you to find your way about these first few days. Just keep quiet. I seem to remember that all one did at first at Ramparts was to keep quiet."

So Bridget, except when she talked about Antosia, kept perfectly quiet until the awful day when Miss Herbert gleamed at her with large, decided eyes behind spectacles and said, "Come with me now, Bridget. You're in my form."

"Oh, but I—"

"Quickly now," said Miss Herbert's firm voice.

It was the Third Form.

With a swelling heart, with tears kept back with fright-ful effort, Bridget went through all the routine of being given a desk, her partner, her books, papers, pens and time-table. This was a thousand times worse than any torpedo. She longed for a sea to come and sweep her away and drown her. She hadn't got into the Lower Fourth, as both her mother and her grandmother had done; she was in the miserable, infantile Third.

The moment the day was over she leapt on to her bicycle and tore back to Green Hedges, tears pouring down her face. It didn't matter who saw them now.

"Oh, Grannie, just listen . . ."

Grannie was sitting over the fire with a book. Tea was on a low, round table with hot scones in a folded napkin, black currant jam, and the cake called Good Useful that Mrs. Drake made once a week. James, asleep in his basket, bounced up in a frenzy of welcome. Rouge got up, stretched himself, wagged his tail, and picked up the fur glove Bridget had thrown on the floor in her desperation. Life became a shade more reasonable and bearable.

"Well, let's hear while you have your tea," said Grannie, and leaned back in her chair, inviting as an open door.

"Hm," she said, when Bridget stopped for another scone. "I expect they don't want to press you too much—after all, everyone doesn't get torpedoed. And there are probably gaps in your education."

"Gaps? I'm all gaps," groaned Bridget. "All the same, the *Third*—they're *kids*. One of them's *ten*. Think, *ten!*"

"Frightful," agreed Grannie.

"I couldn't sort of settle to those papers, I've never done exams. I believe if I did them again, I'd do them heaps better, simply heaps. If only they'd let me."

"Give you a second chance, in fact."

"Yes, if only they would—but they won't."

"You never know."

But Bridget did know. The wheel went round and you went round with it—in the Third Form, with Miss Herbert's eye on you, all among the juniors who talked rot, who didn't use the front stairs, who played rounders. Bridget was again half drowned in despair.

"I'll ring them up and have a talk," said Grannie briskly.

"No good. Miss Herbert wouldn't listen. She's all right, but she doesn't listen much to anyone—she's used to kids."

"I wasn't thinking of Miss Herbert. I meant Miss Adams."

Miss Adams? The Head? The Being who came into Hall for prayers and everyone stood; on whose appearance, wherever it was, silence fell like a dropped curtain; who had three habitations—the Sixth Form Room; a room known as Paradise at the end of a passage that no one was ever seen to enter but which, it was said, was full of flowers and cushions; and a very small and austere room to which you went if you were Sent Up, an appalling event which, if it occurred, darkened your whole term, but which happened mercifully seldom. Grannie couldn't possibly go ringing up *her*.

But the astonishing thing was that Grannie could and

did. She, who trembled before Mrs. Drake, who peeled the potatoes, washed out the dishcloths, scrubbed the kitchen table, and made amiable gossipy conversation when it was the last thing in the world she wanted to do, all to keep the woman in a good temper—she went off to the telephone and called up Miss Adams as if she were the grocer. And had a surprisingly long talk—with laughter in it, too. Bridget took another piece of cake to fortify herself while she listened to the startling sound.

"Oh, she is an amusing card, your headmistress," was Grannie's amazing remark when she came back and threw herself into her big chair to recover from her mirth. "She made me roar."

"But—but did she *say* anything?"

Grannie sat up. She had almost forgotten how serious it was.

"About you? Yes, of course she did. It was only when we'd done with you that we began to laugh. It's all right. She understands perfectly."

"But am I . . . can I . . . do I go on . . . ?"

"You're to go up to the Fourth, Lower Fourth, tomorrow, following the family's footsteps, as I explained to Miss Adams. Tradition, I said, is the making of England, and Bridget is full to the brim with tradition. She says you ought naturally to be there, as you're twelve and no fool—and I'm going to help you with lessons in the holidays. I've guaranteed that you'll catch up, so mind you do. I said you were a tough little body."

"Oh, Grannie, you darling . . ."

James's yelps, Rouge's bass bark, and Bridget's joyful screams all blended together into a chorus of bliss.

> 4 <

Ramparts was a fine big school, old as girls' schools go. Its rightful home was on the outskirts of an East Coast harbor town beside the ghost of its ancient fortifications. Now the war, which seemed to delight in moving nearly everybody and everything elsewhere, had sent it inland to a great house in a park, its hundred and twenty boarders fitted into the big rooms, and its day girls, distributed in the houses and farms round. It wasn't, Bridget's partner told her, at all the same thing, but she didn't mind it.

"Didn't mind it! I should just think not!" exclaimed Grannie when that was repeated to her. "That beautiful old house, its rightful owners squashed into their housekeeper's rooms and a horde of you children given the run of the place—who is your tepid and condescending friend?"

"She's called Violet," said the cautious Bridget.

"Well, tell your Violet to sit up and thank her stars for the marvelous luck that's brought her to Dewhurst Park. And mind you both look at the pictures when you're in that hall. Every possible moment when there's nothing you must attend to, look at them—Romney, Gainsborough, Lely, Holbein, Van Dyck—they're not even names to you yet, but go on looking, soak yourself in them while you can and one day they will be."

But Bridget found very little time for any such soaking. There were only the odd moments when they were all assembled in Hall and for some reason Miss Adams kept them waiting. The rest of the day needed the closest attention, every minute of it. And whenever there was time to spare, Violet buttonholed her and insisted on giving her a lot of information she didn't particularly want about the older girls—which were the ones in for the Certificate and let off games, which were the Sixth who had got it and now lived a life of ease, doing what they liked, who had had a row with whom, who had adored whom for a term and now loathed her, who—

"You're not listening." Bridget was bored to extinction by all this and Violet was naturally offended. "I thought you wanted to be told everything because you were new and so late and all that."

"Yes, I do. But do I have to know all this? I get them all mixed up, and you go on and on—"

"Well, if I'm going to be your best friend—"

"Oh, but you're not, you're *not!*" And the wraith of Antosia would rise up between them, mocking at Violet, with her shiny nose and her mousey hair and her earnest, husky voice giving an absurd importance to all the little things she said—"I was going down the passage to the Sixth and what do you think I saw? Jennifer and that Rhoda girl arm-in-arm, yes, I did—"

"I don't like Violet frightfully," said Bridget to Grannie. "Anyway not after Tossie. I don't know any of the people she talks about and half of them are leaving, so I never shall, and she never stops."

"She sounds like that bore, the school gossip. We used to have them in my day, too. The worst of having had rather an interesting friend like your Antosia—"

"Don't say 'having had.' It isn't 'having had' Tossie for a friend. She *is* a friend."

"Quite so," said Grannie. "My mistake. I only mean that the dull seem duller by comparison."

But however sure Bridget might feel about Tossie and their friendship, there was no getting away from the fact that the stamped postcard that was to bring her new address hadn't come. Time was slipping away like water under a bridge, half term was long past, and there was no word of her. She and her half-uncle had said good-bye, walked down the gangway, and gone off arm-in-arm—turning back to wave a good many times, certainly, but vanishing completely in the end.

"Sometimes I feel as if I'd woken up from Tossie and the boat and all—as if it had never happened," Bridget said.

Grannie promised that one day, perhaps in the Christmas holidays, they would go up to the Polish Legation and make inquiries—but that seemed all wrong, too. You oughtn't to have to go somewhere and make inquiries about your best friend. You ought to know where she is and what she's doing. She ought, in fact, to *write*. Why hadn't she?

No good going on asking questions that can't be answered; you become, Grannie said, almost as much of a bore as Gossip Violet. The thing to do was not to forget Antosia, of course, but just to wait; and meanwhile learn what you could of these perplexing lessons and get on with your hockey. Grannie herself, incredible though it seemed, had once played hockey. She had even been in the Ramparts team. She had been centre half for Ramparts on the occasion when they had beaten the county second eleven, and she still knew how the game should be played. She threw the things off the kitchen table and arranged the field on it with the spoons and forks, herself a large salt cellar as centre half "feeding the wings," as she called it.

"Oh, I wouldn't have been anywhere else for the world. You know everything that's going on, exactly how the game's going. You don't do anything very glorious, you don't dash down the field and shoot goals, but you get hold of the ball, even if you do pass it out to someone with a better turn of speed. But you must learn to *hit*, Bridget. I could hit. Bring back a couple of sticks and a ball and I'll show you." So the next Saturday there they were, running up and down the lawn, with Grannie shouting "Pass" and doing incredibly cunning things with her stick, catching the ball on it, playing cat and mouse with it, cocking up one leg and shooting under it.

"I was rather good as a matter of fact," she panted between her efforts. "I was reserve for the county for a time. Now let's see you dribble it and shoot—now, go on, *shoot*, child!"

The result of all this was a great frenzy for the game on the part of Bridget. She put her name down for every possible practice she could, she watched the forwards of the first eleven being coached, dribbling and passing, the games mistress running beside them in a top coat over her gym dress, just like Grannie only a good deal faster.

Bridget took out a ball and did her best to incite Violet to play a single with her. She had no effect on Violet but very soon when two people went down with chickenpox she found herself in the Lower Fourth team and, though they were beaten in the important match with the Upper Fourth, it was an honorable defeat of four to five and she herself shot one of the goals. It was rather an accident— Grannie wouldn't have called it a shoot at all—she just bundled the ball over the line all mixed up with people's feet. But, never mind, it was a goal and the first she had ever scored in a match, and she strolled back, not with Violet this time but with Eileen, the captain, who told her she'd picked it up pretty quickly, if she'd really never played hockey before and would she play again that day week against the Fifth Second. Oh, *would* she! Very faintly she began to discern what lay ahead, what life at Ramparts could be like when you weren't new any more, when you had learned to be as good as other people at the various things you did. Pretty exciting.

Altogether that was an afternoon to remember; a mild, brown November day, windless and good-natured, the leaves dropping quietly off the trees in their own good time, nothing to hear but the buzz of the tractor in the park, ploughing up the bit that was to grow their potatoes, and an occasional wintry chirrup from the Ramparts robins who were hopeful of worms. It was not at all the sort of day when you'd expect anything to happen; that was why it seemed all the more remarkable that the first thing she heard when she got in from the game was Matron's voice saying, "Bridget, your grandmother has telephoned to say will you hurry up, please. Your Uncle George has come."

Uncle George? Uncle Krak? *Antosia!*

Bridget flew to her bicycle.

TOGETHER AGAIN

Chapter III

➤ 1 ◄

GRANNIE in her oldest tweeds, Uncle George in the comfortable battle dress that made people look so young, were sitting close to the fire, the round tea table between them.

"Do go on. How wonderfully interesting it all is!" Grannie was exclaiming in her warmest voice. "Oh, here's Bridget. Bridget, this synthetic" (now what did *that* mean?) "uncle of yours is telling me about the first jump he ever made as a parachutist and how awful it was. Heavens, the training they get before they're the right mixture of rubber and steel springs—" Then she sneezed— she had a terrible cold—and gave Bridget a chance to ask the question that was bursting out of her—"Where's Antosia?"

Uncle George talked English quite well, in a foreign way that made it sound altogether different and more exciting than usual. Antosia was very well. She had stayed with him for his leave and after that he was doing a course near London and she stayed there, too, in rooms.

"But why didn't she send me the postcard?"

45

"Ah, that was unfortunate—" Uncle George had a charming smile and a way of bowing as he spoke, as if one were grown-up, that was very flattering—"so very unfortunate. She had a coat, you remember—"

"Yes, a green one."

"And she put your card into the pocket of it."

"Yes, I saw her."

"But that coat was very stained and dirty and it was necessary to have another. So we went to buy another and it went to be mended of the sea-water, and alas! the postcard with it. We wrote to the shop but it had gone to Scotland and no one had found the card—Antosia wept for long over that letter. She rang up three people of your name in London but they knew nothing of you. So then we cabled to her father that he might get the address from your father, but he was no longer in India. And then, despair! When what should happen? The coat returned, clean and with the postcard attached to it by a pin. At once I must go. At once—quicker than the post. She could not rest— she would fall ill, she said—so here I am."

"He has come, you see, darling, to find out if Antosia could come down and see you. And of course she shall— some day. We must try to arrange it. Mrs. Drake—poor Mrs. Drake, we shall have to try to persuade her—"

"But where is Antosia now?" asked Bridget. It didn't sound at all like Tossie to send Uncle Krak like this and stay behind herself.

"She—she—well, she is at Shernham." He looked a little abashed, for Shernham was the town close by, their station and shopping place.

"Shernham!" Grannie was decidedly taken aback. "You brought her?"

"Well, yes—or should I say she brought me. She could not bear to wait—it is such a great thing, you see, for her to see her friend, Bridget. I persuaded her to be left at the small hotel by the market. Very restless and determined—"

That was Tossie all over. "She can't seem to settle," the First Officer had said when he brought his boat alongside to ask if Bridget was there.

"I promised I would ring her up." Uncle George grew still more abashed.

"To say she could come, you mean?" Bridget was half-way to the door. "Shall I do it, Grannie? She'll be waiting."

"But, darling—" Grannie sneezed again—"I don't think she *can* come—not tonight, not this very moment—me with this fearful cold—so infectious they are, too. And no time to prepare Mrs. Drake. If she can stay a little longer with her uncle—"

"But that, also, is not possible. My course is finished and I go to Scotland tomorrow."

"Oh, dear, how unfortunate! I don't think I dare—"

Bridget, who knew perfectly well that Antosia would come in the end, began to say that her bed was big enough for two, that Mrs. Drake would be just the same whether she was prepared or not, when the telephone bell rang. "That's her, I bet it is. Shall I say come along?" Grannie was nodding her head and sneezing—it was a sort of assent. . . .

"Hallo, Tossie." Once again Bridget could think of nothing else to say.

Antosia's voice came, half-laughing, half-crying, down the telephone—"Oh, Bridget, I thought I should never see you again!" Exactly what she had said when she was handed over the thwarts and reached her proper place at last.

"Are you coming here?"

"Am I? Oh, *am* I?" She wasn't too sure this time.

"Yes, you are. Have you got your blanket?"

"Yes, I have—and all the stories." And out came a real laugh. "We'll be in the same boat again."

➤ 2 ◄

Grannie took to Antosia from the first moment she came rushing into the room, her blanket over her arm, to kiss her sleeve and cry, "Oh, thank you, thank you, *now* I am so happy!"

Bridget, one of the un-possessive people who want their friends to like each other, stood back and enjoyed the sight. Of course Antosia was bound to love Grannie and the Green Hedges room with the log fire burning, and the kettle singing on the trivet in front of it. with Rouge wagging his tail in greeting and James bouncing up and down in a frantic welcome, with honey for tea in a square china pot with a bee on it; but it was satisfactory the way she took one look and was at home. Very satisfactory. And Uncle George was very soon at home, too. He set himself to make Grannie forget her cold in listening to his stories. His escape from Poland, his adventures, his hardships, the kindness and courage of the people who helped him—it was enthralling.

Antosia egged him on with, "Now, Krak—" (she seemed to have given up the "uncle") "—tell them about the time when you were escaping and you hid for three days up a chimney and the cow wouldn't let you milk her—"

And on he went, his face lightening and darkening, the furrows in his forehead disappearing, making him look a boy, or deepening till he might have been a grandfather. Oh, poor Poland! But what an uncle to have!

Then Grannie's little silver clock chimed and he jumped up, his gaiety falling from him in a moment.

"Now I must go." And he turned gravely to Grannie. "Am I really to leave her?"

"Oh, *yes!*" cried Grannie at once, forgetting Mrs. Drake, forgetting everything in her hospitality.

The little speech he made about gratitude, how Antosia and he would never forget because Poles never did forget either their joys or their sorrows, their loves or their hatreds, how the day would come, he knew, when they would be able to repay a little of the kindness—all this in his queer, broken, yet dignified voice made the tears come into her eyes all mixed up with the sneezes of her terrible cold.

Then he turned to Antosia and made her another little speech, this time in Polish which Bridget didn't understand, but which she guessed by Tossie's shining eyes and nodding head to be about keeping up the reputation of not only her family but of Poland by the marvelously good way she behaved.

After that he said good-bye to them each in turn, took a look around the room, with a little proud nod to it, as if to say, "I'm coming back, you stay here for me," gave them all a little collective bow at the door, and was gone.

"Oh, the magnificent young man!" exclaimed Grannie. "All Poland in the turn of his head—" And she was swept away by a storm of sneezes.

"But with such a cold you should be in bed," cried Antosia.

Of course it was perfectly true, she should. And very soon she was. Tossie, Bridget was relieved to find, was clever in a house. The six weeks she had already spent in England had been in rooms with a brisk landlady who saw to it that she helped in everything. She had learned English ways, English meals, English habits, and she liked them; she intended to like them; the quicker she did so the better, Krak had told her. In no time the two girls had persuaded Grannie to go to bed, lit her fire, filled her hotwater bottle, taken her up supper and her books and papers, and arranged with her to stay in bed the next day.

"You can write all the letters you never do write," said Bridget, knowing what would fetch her.

"But you can't possibly manage," protested Grannie.

"Of course I can with Tossie. Tossie's frightfully good in a house. You see, I'll walk in with breakfast a bit early and then you'll feel nice and strong for Mrs. Drake."

"Oh, Mrs. Drake . . ." She would have moaned if she hadn't sneezed.

That done, the two friends sat down at last to their own supper in the kitchen and had their talk. What a talk it was! All Tossie had been doing, all Bridget had been doing. The hands of the kitchen clock on the wall raced around. Antosia went to bed when she liked—she always had, she said—and anyway, she had no idea of time, as Bridget very well knew.

But Grannie was strict about bedtime—it was half past eight if you were twelve. So Bridget, an eye on the clock, broke off the entrancing conversation and said, "Now then, we must talk about tomorrow. What are you going to do?"

"Going to school with you," said Antosia promptly.

"Oh. But—but I'm not sure that you can."

"Of course I can. Why not? Schools are to go to. Krak has some money for me. I have brought the English school uniform, what our landlady called a gym-dress. She told us about it and Krak and I went to the Army and Navy Stores because that shop has such a tremendous, rolling name, like a cavalry charge, and got it. And all the things that the counter lady said an English schoolgirl should have. Only she was not sure if shoes should be black or brown."

"Ours are brown."

Antosia clapped her hands as if her one anxiety was dispelled. "I guessed brown! I've got brown. So I am complete. I dress in it tomorrow and go with you."

She was so confident, so certain that she would be welcome that for the moment Bridget's qualms disappeared. They couldn't bother Grannie with that cold and anyhow Tossie would go to Ramparts in the end, she'd set her mind on it, so she might as well go now and see what happened. It was a bit irregular as to entrance exams and so on but—Bridget was getting sleepier and sleepier and it was after half past eight, too late to think it out. Tossie was to have her bed, while she slept on the sofa in the sitting room. She'd have to get up before seven if she was to get Tossie off in anything like time; there was only one bicycle and they'd have to take turns, rather a slow business.

"All right, Tossie. Now let's go to bed."

> 3 <

Fortunately James roused up in good time. He was in his basket, but the basket itself was in an unusual place, or else a mouse came out to have a look at him. Anyway, he suddenly woke with a loud, surprised yelp that made Bridget turn on her light and look at the time. Half past six. She lay a moment while the coming day reared up in front of her like a restive horse. Antosia's first day at Ramparts—it was going to take some managing. And Grannie's fearful cold to be dealt with—there was plenty to do before the day could even begin.

Bridget jumped out of her warm sofa and put the kettle on in the kitchen, James yawning and stretching and then leaping beside her. They had laid breakfast over night so the next thing to do was to dress and then call Antosia.

Tossie didn't even wake like anyone else; she kicked and plunged and groaned in a sort of nightmare, then sat up and said, "Where am I?" like a character in a play.

"At Green Hedges," said Bridget sharply. "Get up or you'll be late." And as she said it she knew that was going to be a daily remark. Tossie didn't bother with time.

Grannie's breakfast went up to her, nicely arranged with her letters and yesterday's "Times." Her cold was, if anything, worse. It was working up to its climax, she said, in a cracked ghost of a voice. "Thank you, darling," she croaked. "All so nice. The toast just right. Shut the door after you."

She seemed to have forgotten Antosia's existence. So on the way down Bridget put her head in at Tossie's door and whispered, "Hurry up. I'm beginning. Don't disturb

Grannie, her cold's awful—" because perhaps it would be better if they got off before Grannie remembered that there was such a person as Tossie.

Half past seven. Bridget finished her breakfast, fetched her bicycle and hung her satchel on it. They'd have to go at quarter to eight. No sign of Antosia, so upstairs she went.

Tossie was dressed. She had on a long blue coat, buttoned up to the chin, brown shoes and stockings, and a plum-colored beret on top that looked, for some reason, very French. The beret was wrong but the rest looked all right, and, after all, one didn't wear a cap in school. The room looked as though a tornado had passed through it, with all the contents of two suitcases scattered over the floor, on the chairs and on the writing table where Bridget did her homework.

"Oh, Tossie, Mrs. Drake *dies* if she finds anything about! She's mad about tidiness," cried Bridget, and began to put things away, thrusting them into drawers, boxes, cupboards—anywhere to get them out of sight.

"And who is Mrs. Drake?" inquired Tossie, slightly offended.

"I'll tell you. Go and have breakfast."

"Why should she die at the sight of my new clothes? Why must you hide them—"

In the end, Bridget ran most of the way to Ramparts, with Antosia on the bicycle eating her bread and butter as she went along. Not a soul was about. They were going to be late. Bridget slipped her bicycle into place, changed her shoes in record time, seized Tossie, who was inclined to stare about her and ask questions, and tore off her coat.

"Oh, *gosh!*"

Tossie's uniform was practically red—plum color, like the beret—whereas Ramparts' was navy blue. How awful! How *impossible!* What could she do to hide her? She must go back to Green Hedges at once—

"You like it, Bridget?" Antosia was smiling. "I knew you would. Krak, too, thought it was lovely—my airborne suit, he called it. He gave me his beret to match it. Now what do we do next? It is all so interesting."

She was so pleased, so confident, so thrilled to be at Ramparts that Bridget could say nothing except, "Come on, then."

They were the last two people to come into hall. The hush that heralded Miss Adams had already fallen. Every head turned, every eye stared, round with surprise. Now at last Bridget knew the meaning of that glittering word one met in books but never anywhere else—"cynosure." Antosia was the cynosure of all eyes if ever there was a cynosure. She sat there in her glowing uniform, a ripe plum in a basket of dark blue damsons, and, what was more, she was entirely unconscious of the sensation she made. To her the sensation was Ramparts. So this is Ramparts, she said to herself, gazing round. This is an English school, this long gallery of a hall, these deep windows with the pale light streaming in on the rich jewelled colors of the pictures hanging on the walls, lighting the ruby, sapphire and emerald silks and satins of the portraits—this wonderful place is a *school!*

No one had told Antosia that Ramparts had moved out of its rightful red brick home into one of the ancient and exquisite houses of England. She had spent many months of her life at Warsaw with artistic relations who lived near some picture galleries; she was accustomed to pictures and to people who sat absorbedly in front of them and looked and exclaimed and admired. She now stared about her, enthralled, quite oblivious of the quiet hiss that went around—"Bridget's Polish friend."

They all guessed who she was at once. The way her hair fell forward and was tossed back, the way she walked, the way she gazed at the pictures—none of her was English.

"Polish Antosia," they whispered, and the *ss* rustled through the hall like the stir of reeds when a wind goes over.

Tossie noticed nothing, but Bridget blushed as red as the unique gym dress and thrust the hymn book into her friend's hand with a stern, "Thirty-seven." She could just find her place like anyone else and stop staring at the Van Dyck boy in the lace collar.

"Thank you," said Antosia, much too clearly and composedly, and Bridget blushed anew.

Miss Adams, from her place on the little platform under the Romney Reading Lady in cream-colored satin was near rubbing her eyes. The tall child in red who was giving her a friendly, interested stare ending in a smiling nod —yes, an affable nod—who was she? And what was she doing at Ramparts? No wonder the whole school was fussing and fidgeting.

"Number thirty-seven," said Miss Adams sternly, and set them all off singing.

The new child, Bridget Heath, seemed to be looking after this apparition, trying to keep her in order, nudging her because she couldn't take her eyes off the Van Dyck. She must ring up Green Hedges. One couldn't take in stray

"—this is Antosia, my Polish friend," said Bridget

children like stray puppies, even to please that delightful
grandmother—

Prayers were over, notices were given out. Miss Adams
didn't appear to have seen Antosia. There were ten minutes
before they had to be in form.

"—this is Antosia, my Polish friend," said Bridget, and
half the school clustered around. They knew all about her,
the boat, the ship, the birthday cake with the Polish flag
on it, and she left Tossie to them while she sought out
Miss Elliot, her form mistress.

Miss Elliot had come out of retirement to return to
Ramparts for the duration and do what she called her
war-work, battling with the Lower Fourth. She was
elderly, immensely experienced, an expert teacher guaranteed to make people work who had never worked before.
Generations of Fourths had taught her to be surprised at
nothing.

She began the moment she saw Bridget making her way towards her. "What's all this? Let me tell you I know nothing about this new girl who seems to be with you—*is* she with you?"

"Yes," answered Bridget. "She's—she's my Polish friend."

"Well, I've never heard of her and why she should be sitting with my form at Prayers I can't imagine. Please see that it does not happen again." Cicily Adams (whom she had taught in one of her early Fourths) had no business to go foisting new children on her at the end of term, whether they were Polish or Russian or Double Dutch. "Seven minutes—" she snapped her old half-hunter with a loud report—"and order marks for anyone who's late."

Violet, standing close by—she was always close by—said, "Miss Elliot's going to be in a rage today, you see if she

isn't." Then she added inquisitively, "What form *is* your
Polish friend in?"

"I don't know."

Seven minutes. What did she do now? Ought they to go
and see Miss Adams, both of them? But no one saw her
this time of day. Bridget's mind was spinning. Six minutes
now . . .

"I say—" one of the more sensible people detached herself from the group—"she says she's just come along with
you and no one knows she's here. You can't do that, you
know."

"No. I don't suppose we can," said Bridget unhappily.

"Quite mad. She thinks she'll just sit beside you in
form and drink it all in. She doesn't know Miss Elliot."

"She doesn't know anyone. She ought—I ought—we
ought to have—"

Then Antosia herself came up, tossing her hair back,
still smiling. "Your friends say I should see the one on
the platform, the supreme teacher—"

"No, not *teacher*—"

"—where do I find her?"

"In Paradise," someone said.

"What, suddenly she is dead?" cried Antosia, much
amused, and the first of Tossie's jokes started its travels.

"I *will* not have all this noise." Miss Elliot bustled
back. "This is not the time to laugh in that idiotic way.
Four minutes. Go to your forms, the lot of you."

"You'd better get hold of Miss Adams somehow," murmured the sensible one as she melted away with the rest.

It was all very fine, that "somehow." Everyone had
cleared off and there was Antosia, dancing about the empti-
ness in an ecstasy of joy at what she called Bridget's

"superb" Ramparts.

"But it is beautiful, your school. In Poland our schools have no great pictures. And the girls, they are all my friends already. Now where do we go?"

Where indeed! "I oughtn't to have brought you along like this, I'm afraid—"

But how else could she be brought? Antosia slipped an arm through Bridget's and said it was absurd to frown. They would find the room they so strangely called Paradise. Bridget should introduce her to the lady within who was the chief teacher—no, mistress. Quite simple and delightful. Which way was it?

> 4 <

It was nothing to Antosia to reach the passage and to see the revered door at the end of it; she went dancing down and gave it two smart taps, as though it were a door like any other. "Come in," said a voice, and Antosia opened it to find a leaping fire, a huge jug of yellow chrysanthemums lighting the room, and Miss Adams stretched in an armchair, her feet on the fender, reading the paper.

"Oh, it's you, is it?" said she. "I've been expecting you."

Bridget, in the doorway, shivered at that observation, but Antosia found it a very proper remark. She liked the idea of being expected. She came smilingly forward and put out a hand—the English, her father had told her, shook hands on every possible occasion.

Miss Adams, slightly surprised, shook it and said, "You'd better come in too, Bridget, though I don't think we need shake hands."

"I am so happy to be at your superb school," began Antosia, more "foreign" than Bridget had ever seen her.

"It's not my school. I am the headmistress, appointed by a Board of Governors."

"No matter. Never could I have believed that English girls' schools could be like this, in a so beautiful, rich house with wonderful pictures and painted walls—"

"They aren't," interrupted Miss Adams. "Didn't anyone tell you we are visitors in this house?"

"No," said Bridget, "there was no time—" And out it all came; how Antosia had sent the address to be cleaned with her coat, how Uncle Krak had brought her down only last night, how Grannie was in bed with a cold—no, Grannie didn't know Antosia had come to school. Bridget stood up straight and said all this as clearly and respectfully as she possibly could; they had no business to be at Ramparts, and well she knew it.

Antosia, however, knew nothing of the sort. She didn't even remain standing up. So little did she realize where she was that she knelt down on the hearth rug, holding out her long, slim hands to the warmth, crying that nowhere else on earth would you find such fires. "Only in England are they so open, for everyone, and the flames, blue, yellow, orange, jumping together. But you should have a cat—where is your cat? Always I have seen an English cat to stretch and yawn and curl up and be part of the happiness." She might have been James, she was so sure of herself.

Miss Adams didn't answer about the cat. "I see," she said, when Bridget had finished, "I see . . ." She leaned back in her chair, looking at Antosia, kindly, interested, amused, but critical. Yes, very critical. She had a way of

summing you up, had Miss Adams . . . Bridget grew
anxious as she watched that long look.

"I shall adore Ramparts." Antosia smiled. "Already I
adore it."

"Hm. Yes." Miss Adams considered her further. "But
I'm not so sure that Ramparts will adore you."

"What do you mean?" Antosia threw her head back,
her curtain of hair flying, her face suddenly older; and
there followed, most surprisingly, an argument, an argument as between equals, as to whether she would or would
not fit into the school. Bridget was out of her depth in no
time. Antosia wanted to stay, she wanted it more than
anything on earth. She had fallen in love with the place,
with Green Hedges, with Grannie, and she fought for herself all she knew in three languages. When her English
gave out, she supplemented it with French or her native
tongue, or even a few words of German. She was Polish,
she explained vehemently, she would go back to Poland
the very first moment she could and marry a Polish hus-
band and have a great many Polish children and they
should all speak English and be allies. Her father had said
that she must have an English education and Uncle Krak
said the same thing. She had come from India for that.
She was to be a citizen of the world, not only of Europe,
and to be that she must understand the English, they
both said; and she did understand them, she loved them.
She would be good and studious past all belief. Uncle
Krak had said, "This is perfection where I leave you and
one must deserve perfection." She would deserve it.

"Quite so," said Miss Adams, when at last she could get
in a word. "I see Uncle Krak's point exactly. Nevertheless—"

Her hands, her whole being worked to persuade

Bridget quaked. When Miss Adams said "nevertheless" —a favorite word of hers—there was danger ahead; the whole school knew it. She went on to talk of smaller schools, individual teaching, the heights and depths and gaps of Antosia's knowledge, her upbringing, her age. It was a long "nevertheless" and it meant that Miss Adams did not think Ramparts the place for Antosia.

Tossie's heart was sinking, too, Bridget could see it, though she was fighting as valiantly as ever. Her hair kept falling across her face, her eyes seemed to grow larger, a note of desperation sharpened her voice, her hands waved, her whole being worked to persuade, entreat, reason. Thirteen was not really at all old. She would learn the new lessons, and Bridget would teach her the games and the rules. She would never speak—Miss Adams laughed outright at that—that is, unless she was spoken to.

Miss Adams looked kind and sorry, but her lips were framing another "nevertheless." She didn't think Ramparts was the right school for Antosia; no, she did not. Nothing was going to make her alter her opinion. If she was to be persuaded, it must be by some method, not arguments. Bridget felt she must put in her oar, now or never, or they were sunk.

"You see," she said, in her solid way, "Antosia hasn't got a home or a mother. She hasn't got a country—"

"I have—I have a beautiful country—"

"I mean she hasn't got a country she can get at. She was in the boat with me—"

"What? When you were torpedoed?"

"Yes, that's how we made friends. We were in the same boat."

That blessed torpedo! "We're all in the same boat—well, aren't we?" murmured Miss Adams, almost to herself; and she looked anew at Antosia. Her "nevertheless" began to change into "well . . ." then a much more hopeful "We must see." Antosia's face became a little less strained. Questions and answers of a businesslike nature began to fly and Bridget retired once more into silence. Better. It was going better . . .

In another ten minutes the two girls were outside the door. Antosia was to stay for the day and have dinner and do an entrance paper. Then she was to go back to Green Hedges and not re-appear until the next term. But she was coming to Ramparts. They had won their battle.

They looked at each other in a moment's silence as the door shut. Then "I'm here, I'm here!" Antosia crowed in an ecstasy and seized Bridget's hand to do a dance of joy down the passage.

"No, no—be quiet," whispered Bridget, turning herself into lead, refusing to be dragged. "*Walk*, can't you—" But Tossie couldn't walk; she went caroling along, singing her pet song,

> *"See my chestnut bounding,*
> *Hear her hoofs resounding,*
> *Far on the Orava Road—"*

"Stop it, Tossie. This isn't the Orava Road—"

"Far on the Ramparts Road, then," sang Antosia, and pranced down the corridor to bump into the oldest and most learned member of the Sixth Form, a girl who was already started on her way to becoming a doctor and was carrying a pile of books to the library for a couple of hours of stern biology.

"A thousand million pardons," cried Antosia in French and in English and again in French, to make it sound more apologetic. But it was Bridget who picked up the books and fetched a cloth to mop up the ink, who explained that her Polish friend was in all this hurry because she had an exam to do, the entrance exam for next term.

THE DARLING BULL

Chapter IV

⇥ 1 ⇤

ANTOSIA's voyage had begun. Bridget as her pilot, standing on the bridge in her thick pilot jacket, her cap with its shiny peak pulled well down, was peering ahead. The stormy waters of the morning had been negotiated, Tossie was entered for Ramparts—and a near thing it had been. Now came the tricky waterways of Green Hedges and the floating mine that was Mrs. Drake.

They were on their way back from school, this time Bridget on the bicycle and Antosia, her pockets stuffed with borrowed books, her feet still inclined to skip as if she were bounding along her Orava Road, beside her, holding on to the saddle.

Antosia had had a great afternoon; dinner at the French table beside the ancient Mademoiselle who had been at Ramparts for years and years but who still had her store of jokes and quips and stories from home which seldom got an airing. Antosia had been mothered by a French governess after the English nanny had gone, a Parisian of much the same type and age as Mademoiselle and she understood the jokes, could answer the quips, and supply the right caps to the stories. She enjoyed meeting them all again. And how Mademoiselle enjoyed telling them! Her shoulders heaved, she mopped her eyes with her lacy handkerchief. *"Ecoutez donc—"* And she started on another, and another, and yet again another.

The rest of the table stared. Who was this larky old lady getting off with Bridget's Polish friend? They hardly recognized their bored old teacher who found their accents always atrocious, their remarks stupid, their vocabulary childish in the extreme.

At Bridget's table they were plainly envious. "I say, your Polish friend's pretty good, isn't she? I wish I could talk like that." And Gossip Violet, of course, came out with— Where did she learn? What did her father do? Did she *like* French?—she couldn't. Was she really Polish? If so, why wasn't she black-haired with a big nose? Once more Tossie was a "cynosure," but this time Bridget was proud of it.

After dinner Antosia had done her paper, covering sheet after sheet in her zeal. Her geography was adorned with a wealth of detail about places she had seen with her father, whether asked for or not. "I do not know your history," she wrote at the top of her history paper, "but here is mine—" and there it indeed was, pages of it. She brushed aside questions of grammar, but she did a composition in French, then translated it into English, and had plunged into a German version—a language she was bad at—when she was stopped. Mathematics she left alone—never would she understand a word of them, she said, nor ever wished to— but she was a Shakespearean already. She had seen *Twelfth Night* and *Macbeth* and *As You Like It* with her aunts in

Warsaw and she wrote two pages about Malvolio and how he deserved all he got, and would have written another if time hadn't been up.

"I know a great deal of your education," she said complacently as she trotted beside Bridget.

"You don't. Not half as much as you think. You don't even talk English well."

Antosia laughed and shoved against her so that she ran off the road and sprawled into the hedge. "There. That is all the answer I make. If I have not words, then I must do deeds. A Deed a Day Keeps the Devil Away—my English nanny taught me that."

"She taught you wrong then. It's an apple that keeps the doctor away."

"No, a deed and devil. Look, I pull you back to the road, another deed."

Bridget got on to her bicycle again. "Well, don't you go doing your deeds to me. You keep them for Mrs. Drake."

"Mrs. Drake? Always you talk about Mrs. Drake. Who is she? An aunt?"

"Gosh, no!"

"Why not an aunt? I have very good aunts. Two, in Warsaw."

Bridget explained Mrs. Drake whom Antosia had not yet seen.

"If you're going to really live with us, Tossie—"

"But I am, I am—and this time yesterday I had never seen Grannie, or Green Hedges, or Ramparts—" And out came a stream of Polish that meant "Wonderful!"

"What I was saying," went on Bridget, sticking to the

point, "is that if you are—*as* you are—you'll have to get on with Mrs. Drake."

"But I will. I promise that I will. I will adore her."

"You won't. No one adores Mrs. Drake, except Drake, who's an old angel, and she frightens Grannie out of her life."

At once Antosia bristled up, as she always did if there was the slightest question of bullying. She hated large people, loud voices, authoritative commands.

"But we must not allow it. Be still, Mrs. Drake. Silence! I shall say—"

"You won't. Don't for goodness' sake say anything like that! You'll only make Grannie ill."

"What do I do then to save her?"

"Nothing. Be tidy. Mrs. Drake's a whale on tidiness."

Antosia only groaned.

"And keep out of her way."

"That's easy, easy, easy. I hate her already."

But that was no good either. Keep calm and don't feel anything much where Mrs. Drake is concerned, Bridget wanted to say; but she knew that for Tossie that was impossible. She felt violently, passionately, about everything, from the state of her country to the way her shoelaces would come undone.

"We're late. With any luck she'll have gone."

"I'm glad. Now we go and tell Grannie all the lovely, beautiful news," cried Antosia, skipping up the path.

"No, don't. You sit down and read a book or something and I'll tell Grannie by myself."

> 2 <

Grannie was still in bed, nursing her cold. She was more nearly annoyed than Bridget had yet seen her when she heard what they had been doing.

"I can't have you taking the law into your own hands like this. I really can't. I hadn't the faintest idea what you were up to, walking out of the house like that without a word. I had intended to handle Miss Adams most carefully about Antosia—most carefully. Ramparts is not at all the sort of school that takes just anyone."

"But, Grannie, we did handle her frightfully carefully." And Grannie had to admit that they must have to get such good results. "I only wish I could say the same for myself," she groaned.

"Mrs. Drake, you mean?"

"Yes. I made her get the room next to yours ready—Antosia must have a room to herself, yours is so small. But, oh, dear . . ."

"Awful, was she?"

"Awful! She hardly spoke all day after the first let fly. She came in with my lunch and just stood, looking daggers. It's not the work entirely, she'd heard from Drake that Antosia was a Pole, and that seemed to upset her to the very roots of her being. Now *why* on earth? You'd better go and see how they're getting on—introduce them—do what you can—"

They were not getting on. The first thing Bridget saw was Antosia hunched up on the stairs, just outside Grannie's door. Her eyes were round, her face pink, her hair streaming over it.

Antosia hunched up on the stairs

"She is terrible. Like a Skrzat—"

"Like a what?"

"A Skrzat—I believe she *is* a Skrzat—"

"What's that?"

"A fairy, a real bad Polish fairy who drowns you in the river and throws rocks down on you as you walk about to crack your skull. I am not afraid of her, no, I am not at all, but she pierced me with a terrible look, the look that makes the cows eat the wrong food so that they die. When a baby suddenly cries in its cradle a Skrzat has looked at it—I couldn't stay in that chair and read my book. No, I couldn't. She was pulling my nose and I was screaming—"

"No, you weren't. You're making it all up, Tossie. She didn't touch you and you never made a sound. Be sensible, can't you. Come into the kitchen and shake hands."

"Shake—" Antosia was speechless at the idea.

Bridget took her by the arm and dragged her to her feet, told her not to be silly, but to be sure to say what a nice kitchen it was, and how the pots shone, and that she liked scones. After all, if Antosia was really going to stay, she'd have to get on with Mrs. Drake, and the quicker she began the better.

"No, no, I cannot touch a Skrzat—you English shake hands too much—"

But Bridget, Antosia's arm firmly held, took her down the stairs and threw open the door—on an empty, exquisitely tidy kitchen. The kettle sang gently on the stove, a plate of scones, hot inside their folded napkin, a square of honey, a cake, crowded together on the blue and white checked cloth of the table. A most delicious tea was laid ready for them, in fact. And there were no signs of Mrs. Drake, not even her hat with the bunch of violets on it that she always hung on the door. She had gone.

"There!" cried Bridget. "You and your fairies! Does your Skrzat make you a lovely tea like that?"

> 3 <

"But why—" asked Grannie plaintively when she and Bridget were discussing the situation a few days later, "—why need Mrs. Drake be a fairy at all, good or bad? I don't in the least want either a witch or a leprechaun to run my house for me. Antosia keeps her on the jump somehow. She's always either uttering maledictions about her because something's been left about—and Antosia is quite the untidiest child I've ever met—or making her quite unnecessary jam tarts. You go off to school every day and

you don't see how disturbing it is. I shall be thankful when
term is over and you can help me keep them out of each
other's way."

"It's Tossie being foreign, I suppose," said Bridget cautiously, and went off to have a chat with old Drake, who
came in when he could and did a bit of gardening and who
could generally be found fussing about in the potting shed.
He had some of the quality of the sound, good-natured
brown earth on which his eyes were continually bent, a
sort of fundamental knowledge of people and the world
that Bridget had already found very useful.

"I'm afraid Mrs. Drake doesn't much like my Polish
friend," said Bridget, who believed in saying exactly what
she meant.

Drake was washing flower pots, scrubbing the green off
them with the stump of a floor brush and laying them in
long terra cotta rows. "No, she don't," he agreed, and continued his work.

"D'you know why? Other people do."

"Can't rightly say." He considered a moment, stopping
his washing to wrinkle up his forehead with all its network
of furrows. "The missus, she got to be top-dog, see? Top-
dog an' she'll be all right. But she ain't top, not with a
furriner. Dunno where she be, see? The missus, she don't
like nothing she ain't used to, that's about it, and she ain't
used to furriners."

"But why?"

"Don't rightly know. It's this one belonging up there,
Poland, top of the map, and talking different and all."

"But that's no reason for not liking people."

"That's what I say." Drake took up another pot. Evi-

R.GERMS

"Leave'n be. Give 'em time," said Drake

dently he'd been over this ground a good many times before.

"What shall we do about it?"

"Leave'n be. Give 'em time. She ain't settled. She ain't made her roots yet, the little un. You can't go hurryin'. It'll grow."

"What will grow?"

"Them gettin' on."

> 4 <

It wasn't growing very fast, though, Bridget had to admit, when holidays came and she was all day at Green Hedges. James had to be kept out of the kitchen and now Tossie had to be also. Grannie, she found, sent them out together on some pretext or other the moment Mrs. Drake entered the house.

"Antosia, dear, will you go off to Shernham and get me some soap? We're out of it, I'm afraid. And would you take James? So good for him." Every morning as the latch of the back door clicked, Grannie made this or some similar request, and Tossie, anxious to oblige, anxious to do anything to show how good she was being, hurried off. "No, don't hurry," Grannie would call after her, then turn back into the house with relief.

"But, Grannie, Tossie's so good in a house," Bridget expostulated. "She did a lot at home and a lot in those rooms with Uncle George. She rather likes it."

"I know, but Mrs. Drake won't let her. It's absurd, but she won't. Everything Antosia does Mrs. Drake undoes or does all over again—and then she'll make a cake and put it in her bedroom. It's she who thinks Antosia a fairy, not the other way round. She's half-afraid of her."

Bridget nodded wisely. That was Mrs. Drake buying herself into the position of top-dog, as she couldn't get there any other way, paying for it with jam tarts and cakes. And Tossie never even said thank you, merely brought them downstairs again and put them on the table with everything else.

"Mrs. Drake doesn't like what she's not used to," Bridget explained, quoting Drake, who must know why she did these things, if anyone did. "She's not used to foreigners."

"Ridiculous! The whole island's full of them," cried Grannie impatiently. "She belongs to a hundred years ago, silly insular old thing. Oh, why can't I cook! How can I learn with everything rationed and nothing to spare for mistakes." And Grannie would shrug her shoulders de-

spairingly and go off on one of the hundred and one jobs
she was always doing.

It'll come, Drake had said; but the "getting on" that he
had predicted was taking a long time to begin. Here they
were in the third week of the holidays and there was no
sign of it.

"The Skrzat hates me," Tossie would say cheerfully.
"She never looks at me but always to one side, as if someone walked beside me. She sniffs when I speak, as if there
was a bad smell. She would like to kick me as she kicks
poor James when I come into the kitchen. Let her hate me.
Poles can hate, too."

"Now don't you go saying that."

"Why not?"

Antosia looked surprised. "But if a person hates you,
you must hate them back."

"You needn't. You needn't think about them at all."

"Be like James, you mean?"

"Yes, like James. Keep out of her way and forget her."

But Antosia was unconvinced, and things went on the
same. In fact, the settling down together that Drake was
so confident about might never have happened at all, if it
hadn't been for an earthquake that, so to speak, tore up
Mrs. Drake by the roots, tossed her into the air, and
brought her back again to earth an altogether different
person.

➤ 5 ◄

A couple of fields separated the back of the Drakes'
house and the back of Green Hedges. Both belonged to a
farmer. He made no difficulty about the path which Drake
and Mrs. Drake made as they went backwards and for-

wards by this convenient short cut from one back door to the other. Occasionally, however, he used these fields for a bull that had for some reason or other to be left by himself for a bit. When that happened he rang up Grannie and told her, and Drake, who was old and slow, invariably took the cautious way and came round by the road. Mrs. Drake, however, never did any such thing. No bull, she said, was going to make her waste half the day traipsing round all that distance (she hardly went out of her house except to go to Green Hedges). So she stuck to the fields, waited for the moment when the bull was in a distant corner, then over she went, walking rather faster than usual as a concession to his presence.

They were a harmless enough lot of bulls as a rule. The day came, however, when a young, hot-tempered, newly-acquired animal, who had traveled in a trailer horse box and hated it, spent his first day in his new home in the larger of the fields, the one nearest Green Hedges. He didn't like the place, the journey had worried him, there were no cows about to keep him contented, and he was ready to be in a rage about almost anything. The cape flapping in the wind, the shine of white apron below, the "browned off" feeling he suffered from, all combined to make him hate Mrs. Drake at sight. Here's the creature that's at the bottom of the whole thing, he said to himself. He stood there, lashing his tail and himself into a fury until she was halfway across. Then he began to paw the ground, sending the earth shooting up in a shower of little clods that came down on his own back and excited him still further, and gave a long bellow.

At that bellow Mrs. Drake, who had been perfectly conscious of him the whole time, though she daren't turn round, began to run towards the gate into the next field, sideways, looking back at him, like a particularly clumsy crab hurrying over rocks. "Oh, my! Mercy! He's comin'! Archie—" Archie was Drake's Christian name, only used on rare occasions.

But her little squeak of a voice didn't carry. Drake was at that moment sitting by the fire, a newspaper over his face, enjoying forty winks before his dinner. No one heard her except the bull. The little chirruping noises made him feel angrier, also very triumphantly victorious. He fixed his little reddened eyes on her and thundered towards her . . .

"Mercy save us!" sobbed poor Mrs. Drake, her heart thumping like a hammer, every breath turning a knife in her breast. A touch and she'd fall down—the world was turning black, red stars shot across her eyes. She ran faster, stumbling, panting, groaning. She'd never reach the gate before he got her. She'd never open it if she did. She was going to be killed. "Archie, Archie boy—" She hadn't called Drake that for forty years. But Drake never heard.

Someone else, however, if she didn't hear her, heard the bull.

Antosia, on her way back from Shernham, where she had been buying Grannie another of these endless half-crown stamp books, heard and recognized his bellow. In Poland, where her father bred his horses, they had a farm. It didn't often happen, but if a bull lost his temper, that was the noise he made; and there was a bull in the field behind Green Hedges—as it happened she had taken the telephone message about him herself.

"Come on, James," she cried, and broke into a run up the last hill, in a hurry to see if anything exciting was going on. A few yards ahead there was a gap in the hedge that allowed her to see those two fields.

Something going on? Indeed there was! One look and she tore down the road, into the Drakes' cottage, out at the back door (in Drake's dream a large dark bird flew, flapping and screaming, past his head) pulling off her coat as she ran. James, ready for the new game, yelped and jumped at her heels.

She reached the gate just as Mrs. Drake fell, scrambled up, and fell again. "I'm coming, I'm coming, Mrs. Drake—" she shouted, and got the thing open—it had to be lifted slightly and a hook and chain adjusted. The bull, who had charged and unaccountably missed—the creature's shape changed and flattened to the ground just as he was going to toss it—bellowed again. Then he found something soft and dark over his head, blinding him, suffocating him. He threw up his heels to shake it off; but it was Antosia's coat, and one of his horns stuck in a sleeve. He went careening off, angrier than ever, trying to toss the clinging horror that muffled his bellow and blinded his eyes and maddened him altogether.

"Get up, get up!" cried Antosia, but Mrs. Drake, half-conscious, could only open and shut her mouth and gasp like a fish, her eyes tightly closed. It wasn't the bull, it was the foreigner, the Polish girl who gave her the shivers, who'd been chasing her across the field—and who'd now got her. She gave up all hope. There wasn't even breath for a groan.

"There's only a minute—he'll get it off in a minute—" And Antosia seized Mrs. Drake under the arms and began to drag her into safety. She was a small woman, but solid, and a dead weight because she was now frightened into a

Antosia seized Mrs. Drake under the arms

faint. Tossie was strong, however, and, conscious or not,
Mrs. Drake was pulled through and the gate shut again
before the bull finally tore the coat to ribbons through
which he caught a glimpse of the little white thing that
yelped and barked and bounded around him. So you did
it, did you? James, too young to be wise, thought it just
another game, but he was soon disillusioned about that.
Poor James, he missed being tossed by a hair's breadth, and
ran, yelping a very different tune, as fast as his legs would
carry him back to home and safety, the bull after him.
There was a hole in the fence, he knew, and he streaked
off to it, reaching it and diving through with the horns a
yard from his back, never slackening until he was in Green
Hedges, up the stairs, and under Bridget's bed.

Grannie had seen most of this from her bedroom
window.

"Bridget, the bull's after Mrs. Drake. Fly and get Drake.
Go round by the road—the *road*, mind. I'm coming."

But she wasn't coming because at the moment she happened to be changing. All she could do was to hurry all she knew. She flung her clothes on, one eye on the bull, the other on Mrs. Drake's little square figure. "Oh, my goodness . . ." she half-groaned, half-shuddered, half-cheered, when Antosia appeared. "Courage—Poles have such courage . . . look at her!" Then came the coat flung over the bull's horns and she heard herself give the most strange, exultant crow of joy—"She's done it! Oh, the marvel . . ." She seized smelling salts and brandy and dashed off, her skirt kept on by one hook, her shoelaces trailing, her hair flying, but pulling on her enormous gloves.

➤ 6 ◄

Mrs. Drake had been got to her kitchen by the combined efforts of Antosia, Bridget and Archie boy. A cup of strong tea with plenty of sugar in it was slowly reviving her, clearing her mind, bringing back to her what really had happened. She looked, amazed, at the green stains on her apron, at the mud on her hands; she felt her head—the hat with the violets that she had worn for eight years was gone. So it wasn't the foreigner who had chased her across the field, like a young witch with a broomstick, and made her run and fall down and then run and fall down again; it was that bull. The foreigner—and there she was, chattering away to Drake this minute—the foreigner had saved her life, pulling her through that gate. Yes, so she had.

Mrs. Drake reached this conclusion, holding Archie boy's hand as she hadn't held it for forty years, just as Grannie came in. A teaspoonful of brandy in her tea loosened her tongue and lit up her mind still further, and she talked as they had never before heard her talk. Bridget listened, astonished; but old Drake wagged his head knowingly, as if this was just what he'd expected.

"I'll never say another word against foreigners, not Poles nor nothing else, not were it ever so. Thought she was a witch, I did. She fair gave me the creeps with her jabber and doing things so airy and belonging to goodness knows where up north, but she come across that field like an angel from heaven. She did truly, and saved me life. Thought I was gone—that great elephant behind me—" And Mrs. Drake panted, turned sick, and closed her eyes at the memory.

"Now don't you go off again, Mrs. Drake!" cried Antosia, warningly.

"It's all right, missus. Safe enough now," said old Drake, soothing as a lullaby, and he gave her hand a heavy pat, as if he were settling in a young plant.

"I saw it all," said Grannie, most flatteringly flustered. "My heart was in my mouth, it really was. I nearly swallowed it when I saw Antosia come flying along. What made you think of the coat, Antosia? I can't imagine how you had time to think of anything."

"Saved my life, she did," repeated Mrs. Drake, now inclined to sob.

"Oh, no, Mrs. Drake, it was James who did that. The bull went after James instead of us." Antosia insisted that James was the hero. Poor James, where was he? The coat was lying in strips and tatters about the field and the bull was still roaming around, giving bellows that grew milder and milder, but there was no sign of James.

"He's under my bed, you bet," said Bridget, and, as

there was nothing more they could do for Mrs. Drake, off
they went to Green Hedges to entice James out with the
largest bone they could find, and tell him what a clever
dog he'd been. Poor James! He kept close to heel even
when passing a cow from that day forward.

It was a week before Mrs. Drake was sufficiently recovered from her bruises to make the journey between her
house and Grannie's, and during that time they cooked
for themselves. They all cooked. Antosia was the best at
it; she made them "Little Doves," which turned out to be
odds and ends of meat rolled up in cabbage leaves, and
the famous beetroot soup, which was certainly very good.
Grannie, with Bridget reciting the recipe over and over
again, like an incantation, tried all sorts of things, some of
them delicious, some very nasty, but all hopefully and
tactfully eaten. Bridget spent her time washing the pots
and pans and sometimes got as far as making scones and
frying pancakes.

"The Skrzat will soon be back," said Antosia one day.

"Yes, I'm afraid she will," groaned Bridget. It was fun
doing the cooking with Grannie, who got a thrill out of
every meal.

But Tossie only smiled.

"She will be better. Not any more a Skrzat, perhaps.
Now she will be a Baj."

"What's a Baj?"

A special fairy for children, apparently, who played the
fiddle and crept across the ceiling when they were in bed,
bringing them bunches of poppies and ears of corn.

"But we are too old for that," said Tossie. "This Baj
will bring us something else. You wait."

She did. She arrived with Drake behind her carrying a

basket wherein was a pot of her best strawberry jam, a cake, and the last of her bottled cherries. And, what was more, a bone for James and an invitation to come into the kitchen as often as he pleased. As for Antosia—well, there was no more hurrying off to Shernham to buy stamps no one wanted, the moment the latch of the back door clicked. Everything Tossie did or said was perfect.

"That *darling* bull!" said Grannie, sighing with relief. "He's made another woman of Mrs. Drake."

ANTOSIA AT RAMPARTS

Chapter V

➤ 1 ◄

THE holidays came to a cheerful end and Antosia's first day at Ramparts loomed ahead. As a preparation for it the air-borne suit had been dyed dark blue.

"No good keeping it," Grannie explained when Antosia disapproved of this. "It's none too big as it is and I can almost see you grow."

"But that color is so dull. Uncle Krak's beret—"

"Ramparts wears blue, you see."

"But why should *I*? I like red. Why should we be the same? I like sometimes to be different, I will put 'Poland' on the sleeve—"

Grannie and Bridget explained together. It was uniform; and the point about uniform is that it's uniform. "Everyone looks the same," said Bridget, "and that's a good thing."

"Why is it a good thing?"

"Oh, well, like soldiers, you know." Bridget was vague, she had never given it a thought.

Fortunately, vague or not, that satisfied Antosia. "I

see. Ramparts is our regiment." She nodded her head, as if understanding that well enough, and threw herself into the business of joining up with the greatest energy. She had never been to school, even in her own country, and she had everything to learn about such places.

Bridget, after a term there, felt an old hand, specially after the work in the holidays, which had let her catch up with the rest of the form. "You stick to me, Tossie," she said, "and I'll tell you exactly what to do. Ellie wants knowing, but she's all right. She was ratty that day because I took you along to her form without asking her. Don't you worry."

But when the day came there was no sticking to Bridget, for Antosia was not in the Lower Fourth, she was in Remove.

Bridget turned away from the notice board in amazed horror.

"*Remove?* You can't be!"

Antosia, however, showed no signs of worry.

"Why can't I?" she inquired.

"No one is. It's full of duds and freaks and geniuses. There's Rosemary Parke who's had typhoid, and that French girl, Toinette, who's learning English, and Elspeth MacDonald who's been away for two terms, and Judy who has to practice three hours a day *and* lie down. They're all absolutely rotten at things or too frightfully good for anything."

"I shall like that," said Antosia, and went off, smiling, to her duds and freaks.

It was a good thing, Grannie said, a very good thing that Antosia was in another form. She and Bridget didn't want to sit in each other's pockets all day; they saw quite enough of each other at Green Hedges. "It's nothing to be disappointed about. She'll bring back different ideas and stories and have different friends. Very likely they'll be a most interesting collection of girls. Excellent."

But Gossip Violet said nastily, "Sickening for you, not having your Polish friend. Nothing but poor me for a partner. What does her father do? You never told me. Is he rich? What did her mother die of? Why has she come to England? Does your grandmother really like her? And who's she going to have as her special friend in that form—she and Toinette aren't supposed to talk French, but I believe I heard them—"

Yes, it was pretty sickening. Bridget had been looking forward to having Tossie as her partner instead of Violet. However, there were still a good many things they could do together; hockey, for instance. Remove didn't have a hockey team, they were attached as individuals to different forms and games according to their age and size, and luckily Antosia was attached to the Lower Fourth.

She found it a most confusing and annoying game.

"I think I shall not play hockey," she announced after her first attempt at it in a very minor practice game. "Tennis, yes. I played tennis with my father in India. Hockey, no."

"Bunk, Tossie," said Bridget, who had been in a different, much more superior game. "Of course you'll play. You'll be jolly good at it because you can run. What's the matter with it?"

Tossie shrugged her shoulders and spread her hands in her foreign way. "A girl—it was your friend Violet—hit the ball hard so that it hurt my ankle and I ran after her to hit it back at her to hurt her ankle more. It did hurt her

much more and the mistress, she blew a whistle and everyone stood still. The mistress said to me, 'You could be
ordered off the field for that,' and I said, 'But if she hits
me, I must hit her back.' And she said, 'No, it's a foul,'
and I said, 'Is it then a game for hens?' and everyone
laughed. Oh, how easily they laugh!"

"Well, I should have laughed, too. What happened
then?"

"Then we started again and we all fought together for
the ball, like dogs fighting for a bone, and I got it. Could
I keep it and run away with it to the goal? No! 'Pass,'
cried the mistress, and I have to give it up to someone else.
Why?"

"Well, you see . . ." and Bridget tried to explain the
principles of the game. You passed out because left wing
was there with a clear field and could get away with the
ball better than you could. She passed back because centre
forward had a better chance to shoot, and so on and so on.
Everyone in fact played as well as the next person let
them."

"But I don't see," cried Tossie, when Bridget had finished. "My father says you must play a game to *win*. I
like to win by myself. I hit, you hit, I hit harder, you hit
harder, I hit hardest of all—I win. That's what I like."

"But you do play to win—" Bridget didn't try to explain
any more. When they got back to Green Hedges they
went out into the garden with hockey sticks and an old
ball. She put up goal posts of a couple of flower pots, and
they played singles, with Grannie shouting encouragement
and advice out of the window. Antosia was, as Bridget had
prophesied, good at it. Her longer arms and turn of speed
soon made her the winner in the sort of beggar-my-neigh-

bor games they had up and down the lawn. Nevertheless, there were countless times when Bridget got the ball away from Tossie and "passed" to an imaginary player on her left, or when Grannie cried, "Diddle her, Bridget, diddle her!" and by some magic with the point of her stick the ball disappeared.

After that game Antosia began to like hockey rather better. She came back one Saturday to announce at supper, "I shall play left wing," as if she had at last made up her mind about something.

"Quite right. Find the place you like and go for it," said Grannie. "But you'll have to be fast. Bridget's going to play centre half because she likes to know what's going on."

Sure enough, as the term wore on, Miss Harrison, the games mistress, was heard to say, "She's got the making of a forward, that Polish child. Let's try her outside left."

Antosia was tried in a superior game, and with Bridget passing out very often, feeding her cleverly, she made two spectacular runs that got them two goals, centering beautifully for one but shooting the other herself I¹ wasn't an important game but Miss Harrison was there watching, and when the Fourth Oxford vs. Cambridge match came on the two friends found themselves elected to play for Oxford, Bridget for centre half, Antosia for left wing.

"That's right," said Grannie, very pleased, when she heard the news. "You're both on the ladder. Up you go."

> 2 <

Cricket, when the summer term came, was easier to explain, but harder, much harder, to do. Antosia liked it.

She thought the fall of the wicket, the walk out alone when you went in, the way the stumps were drawn and it stopped dead in an instant, all very dramatic.

"I could turn it into a dance, a very serious, lovely dance, all white and green," she said. She was thrilled with the moment of going in to bat, but once there, having gone through the ritual of taking middle-and-leg and all the rest of it (she wouldn't miss out a word), try as she would, she never made any runs. She lashed out at every ball, giving a slight hiss like a serpent, invariably missing it, until at last a straight one came, and down went her wicket. She greeted that with a sharp, despairing cry, in Polish, and crept back in a shamefaced way to the pavilion, having enjoyed every moment of her innings. If her partner hit a good one and cried, "Come on," she ran, panting with excitement, past the crease, past the wicket keeper, on for yards and yards, as if winning a race, so that there was never a hope of a second run. And nothing could make her bowl. She never remembered to stay behind the crease, and when it wasn't a no-ball for that reason it was one for flinging the ball at the batsman's head. She made the game great fun—"How easily you English laugh!" she often had occasion to say—but she never found her way into any eleven. "And I never shall," she cried cheerfully. "But I adore it. It is fun. It is fun-and-games. Now tennis, that is serious—that is a very serious game at which one never laughs."

And as played by her it was. Her father was a fine player and she had been well taught. She went on to the courts, her face preoccupied and tense, a small, set frown between her eyes, and I'm-going-to-win in every line of her. And it was amazing how often she did win, even against girls a great deal older and bigger than herself.

"By next year she'll be in the Eight, see if she isn't," declared Miss Harrison after watching her, the score five to one against her, drag it up to five-all and then take the set from an amazed Upper Fifth who thought she had won long since. And when the handicap American tournament began, Miss Harrison gave Tossie a big one that kept her full stretch whoever her opponent might be. "That'll be good practice. Antosia will never see the inside of any cricket eleven on earth, but, you wait, she'll be playing the tennis singles for Ramparts one day, and winning them, what's more."

> 3 <

Antosia adored her funny Remove. Grannie was quite right when she said they'd probably be a very interesting lot. They were, Tossie declared; far more so than Bridget's old Lower Fourth. She had no very particular friend among them; she took them all in turn, and, according to her, each one was more remarkable and fascinating than the last. It was generally at suppertime that the revelations came out.

"Elspeth MacDonald—now did you ever guess for one moment that she was Scottish?"

"Of course I guessed," said Bridget. "With that name, what else could she be?"

"But you didn't know she had an ancestor who took their king in a small boat, rowed him away, and saved him." Antosia's eyes were bright with admiration.

"Flora MacDonald and Prince Charlie—speed, bonny boat like a bird on the wing—everyone knows that story."

"Ah, but what you *don't* know is that Prince Charlie's

mother was a Pole. She was Clementina Sobieska. And you mustn't say 'prince,' he was their king—their king over the water. When I heard that, we were friends at once. Naturally. Listen—" Antosia dropped her voice and leaned across the table. "We are starting a secret society. You can't join it because you are English, but—"

"A secret society," said Grannie, cheerfully, "but how interesting! What for?"

"To restore the Scottish king, of course. In Poland everyone joins a secret society. My aunts in Warsaw each belong to different ones—they have for years and years. One of them was chased through the forest by Cossacks, she fled away on the back of a motor bicycle—bumping and bumping. Once when my other aunt gave a tea party they put me outside the door to give warning if anyone came—"

"But why shouldn't they come if it was a tea party?"

"It wasn't. It was a meeting. I was a sentry. They were disguised, many of them. Some had been in prison—they'd bribed the guards and got out, or they'd sawed through bars and slid down the walls—"

"Oh—" Bridget blinked. Here was a glimpse of another world altogether, a terrible world of disguises, prisons, escapes, people who chased you, and Tossie had lived in it—or on the edge of it.

"But, Antosia," Grannie now leaned across the table, too, "we don't go in for secret societies in this country. There's not the necessity, thank heaven."

Antosia looked at her almost sternly.

"But you yourself belong to one—of course you do. Bridget is too young and I am a stranger, we must be told nothing. That is right, for they are secret."

"But I don't."

"You wear a uniform, a badge—"

"That's the W.V.S. There's nothing in the least secret about it. It's a nice, sensible, comfortable suit, a good serviceable color, far more becoming than most of my clothes, and I'm forever doing odds and ends for them. I'm not sure that Miss Adams will be too keen on secret societies at Ramparts. Heads of schools—"

"Heads? Always you must fight heads. You must rebel. Again and again I have heard my aunts say that."

"But I thought Miss Adams had been such a friend."

"Yes, she has." Antosia was a little confused.

"Well, what I mean is, I'm sure she'll think it a great waste of time and energy with all these exams and things in front of you."

"But in Poland, in my country, it is our first duty to rebel."

"Hm—" Grannie grew milder and milder. "But it's different here. You bring your Elspeth to tea and we'll talk about Scotland and Poland and you'll see just how different they are."

"As a matter of fact, I don't suppose anyone would mind," Bridget broke in, trying to be tactful. "They do have secret societies at Ramparts, I believe, pass words and all that. But it's the Third Form—"

"The children— Oh, Bridget, if you only knew!" And Antosia covered her face with her hands.

"Have some more pudding," said Bridget, to end this uncomfortable and most perplexing conversation. But Tossie only shook her head, and when, after a few minutes, she looked up Bridget was amazed to see there were tear stains on her cheeks. Well, well, well. No good asking why;

there were a lot of things in Antosia she could never share, and this mysterious grief was one of them.

> 4 <

But Bridget had to wait until the end of the summer term before Antosia really showed Ramparts what she could do; before people like Sixth came up and said, "Your Polish friend's a marvel, she really is," and she could glow with pride and agree, "Yes, isn't she!"

There was to be no big play, owing to one thing and another, but every form had to produce some sort of entertainment lasting twenty minutes, and the best of them, if they were good enough, would be polished up and performed at a big breaking-up party.

"Remove won't do an entertainment," said Bridget. "They've had this kind of show before and they say Remove never does."

"Who's 'they'?" asked Antosia, and tossed back her hair.

"Oh, everyone. Too few of them, I s'pose. Oh, Tossie, couldn't you come into our form for that? You could do one of your dances—"

But Antosia skipped off, saying she'd talk to Remove. "They" were going to be wrong this time. Bridget could just wait and see how wrong. There were nine people in Remove. Plenty, plenty, plenty.

Grannie, when she heard all this, said Antosia was perfectly right. Numbers weren't everything. She wouldn't be at all surprised if Remove, goaded on by Tossie, wasn't as good as any of them. She hoped she'd be there to see it.

"But you won't be, Grannie. Only the frightfully super

ones get to the party. I don't suppose you'll see either of us."

Bridget, in fact, was gloomy about the whole thing. She had a good idea of acting herself and their own play, she knew, was dull as ditchwater. It was about Robin Hood and it ought to have been exciting, but it wasn't. People were keen enough, there was very little prompting; but they were all exactly the same, all speaking so politely, no one saying a word as if they meant it, all so *stodgy*. Now if they could have got hold of Tossie as Maid Marian instead of Violet . . .

Sure enough, there was Remove's name up on the board with the others, the title of their entry in block capitals—VARIATIONS.

"What sort of thing is it you're doing with your lot, Tossie?" Bridget couldn't help being curious. "Is it a play? What's it about?"

" 'Surprise is an important element in drama,' " quoted Antosia, in Addy's exact accents. She was a good mimic.

"Is it a skit on all the mistresses, because if it is—"

"Wouldn't you like to know!"

No one was supposed to ask questions; the idea was to keep everything dark until the actual day. But Bridget couldn't help cautiously probing.

"You don't seem to be bothering much about clothes."

"Toinette is very clever," Antosia answered airily; and that was all she would say. When Grannie asked how were the duds and freaks and geniuses, she replied that they were all geniuses now, and melted away by herself into the kitchen garden to do some mysterious practice, jumping off a frame, dancing up and down the path, and then skipping up again.

A certain amount leaked out about the other forms, but no one had the ghost of an idea what Remove was doing. No one had seen Antosia or anyone else put a stitch into anything, and they went into the wood at the back of the house to rehearse.

The day drew near. Each group had a private hour and a half in the hall for rehearsal, then they drew numbers out of a hat for their places on the program. The Lower Fourth came first of all; Remove last.

"I don't like either of those places much," grumbled Bridget, who was rather strung up. "We'll be duller than ever if the audience haven't warmed up, and by the time you come, Tossie, they'll be stale, fed up."

"Then we shall un-feed-up them," cried Antosia, cheerful as a lark. "But, oh, how I long to begin!" She wrung her hands together and skipped away.

The day came. Miss Adams's platform had been enlarged and the Romney covered with a blue curtain. The audience sat not in rows, but as they liked, on the floor, with their own rugs and cushions, with a few odds and ends of chairs for mistresses and other people who wanted them. In the intervals they walked about and exchanged opinions. The last performers came in to join the audience while the future ones went out to get ready. Two judges from outside the school sat sharing a small table at which they wrote their criticisms; very important people these were whose business it was to decide which two entertainments should be given at the party.

The Lower Fourth began. It was, as Bridget knew it would be, very dull. The audience knew Robin Hood and this particular story about him rather too well, and the acting was not good enough to make it live again for them. However, it was a harmless show, all right as a beginning. They gave the performers a good-natured clap, then got up to stroll around and discuss the next, the Sixth.

The Sixth had a girl whose parents were both on the stage, and they were doing the trial scene from *The Merchant of Venice* with her as Portia. It was bound to be pretty good, everyone thought, because Lavinia must have heard her mother in the Quality of Mercy speech dozens of times. The audience expected a great deal, and they got it. When the scene came to its impressive end, they clapped respectfully and enthusiastically. It was *marvelous*, they told each other, and it would be one of the two winners for certain. And the other? Well, that was now the interest. Rumor said the Lower Fifth had a frightfully funny play with a charwoman in it, and it was coming next. The audience got ready to laugh, but unfortunately there was nothing much to laugh at, and the judges never smiled for an instant. Bridget thought she saw one of them write a round "o" in the space marked "Choice."

The Upper Fourth came next, with another pretty silly play about a jumble sale and the judges didn't think much of that, either; also, rather too much of it was said by the prompter. The Upper Fifth, last but one, had been a bit too ambitious. They did a musical play, but it needed more time, more clothes, proper producing (Bridget overheard one of the judges say that). It was a good shot at it, but it wasn't more than a shot.

"I can't see Addy allowing that as a show-off," the Lower Fourth captain murmured. "We aren't so bad, after all." They weren't. There was only Remove to go.

"We could ginger ours up," Bridget whispered back, already busy with plans to get in Antosia. "If Violet's cold isn't better, a lot better, she can't do Maid Marian—she sneezed eight times, enough to put off anyone—"

Remove began.

The curtain went up on an empty stage. Then in ran Antosia, very happy and smiling in her Polish dress, white bodice with big sleeves and gay striped skirt—all the colors of Poland's long strips of fields in summer. She gave a little curtsey to the audience. Remove proposed to remove them to Poland, she said, for twenty minutes and she hoped they would enjoy their visit. They would begin with the Robbers' Dance that was always danced before a Polish wedding; the Robber would be killed and they would visit every house in the village for things to bury with him; but they need not fear—once in his grave, he would revive, and their gifts would be returned to them. It was extraordinary, as Bridget told Grannie when trying to describe Tossie, the way she made the audience feel that she was enjoying herself, and that they would enjoy themselves because something really delicious was going to be put before them.

Then Judy appeared, looking entirely unlike herself in white trousers and embroidered coat, tied round her neck with a cord, the sleeves hanging empty, like a cape. She sat down at the piano and plunged with immense verve into the dance. She was quite startling. Of course they knew she practiced three hours a day and was supposed to be pretty safe for a scholarship at the Royal College— still, they never thought she could play quite like that. Gosh! Tossie *has* been after her, Bridget said to herself.

Tossie had been after the others, too. Rosemary Parke, who wasn't allowed to dance, was the Robber. She was

quickly despatched, and lay most conveniently on the stage
while the others, two and two, white trousers with striped
shirt, danced off the platform (so that was what Antosia
had been practicing, skipping on and off the frame in the
garden), in and out of the groups on the floor, and took
handkerchiefs, a shoe, a belt, a brooch, a book, anything,
from them, and danced back to the "corpse." They seized
the dead Robber to put him into his grave and up came
Rosemary, as alive as anyone, and it all ended with a
glorious whirling crash.

Instantly there was another crash—applause. Everyone

It all ended with a glorious whirling crash

sat up and clapped, not respectfully this time but as if they'd had quite a shock. "It's the *vitality*—" murmured one judge to the other. How did she make them smile like that and look so gay? Remove weren't particularly gay. Where did she get the clothes? Borrowed? Yes, Remove had been getting a lot of parcels, now that they came to think about it. "Pretty marvelous," said one of the Sixth. Bridget beamed, and saved it up for Grannie.

Then the dancers sat around Antosia and she told them a story. It was a story Bridget knew well; the first time she had heard it they were under the blanket in the boat. It had been Bobby White's favorite. When Tossie changed her voice for all the different animals he could always laugh, even when he was turning into the poor little thin gnome and was almost too tired to listen.

In the beginning God gave all the animals their food. The wolf came to Him and said, "What shall I eat?"

God said, "You may eat bread."

"Where shall I find it?" asked the wolf.

"You'll have to grow it. First you plough the land."

"And then do I eat?"

"No, the grain will shoot and grow."

"Then do I eat?"

"No, when the corn is ripe you must reap it."

"*Then* do I eat?"

"No, you must thresh the corn."

"And *now* can I eat?"

"No, you must take it to the mill and grind it."

"Now can I eat?"

"No, you must make bread and bake it, and then you can eat."

"Much too slow," said the wolf. "*Far* too slow. Give me something else."

"All right, you can eat meat."

"But where shall I find it?"

"Over there is a mare and foal. Eat the foal."

So the wolf went off to the mare and said, "God says I may eat your foal."

The mare said, "Very well, take him by the tail and try."

So the wolf took the foal by the tail and the foal kicked him in the mouth and knocked a tooth out.

The wolf went back to God and said, "I don't like the

foal you gave me to eat. Give me something else, please."

"All right," said God. "There's a ram on that hill, you may eat him."

So the wolf went off to the ram and said, "God says I may eat you."

"All right," said the ram. "Only don't go eating me in little bits, eat me whole. Much better."

"How do I do that?"

"Listen and I'll tell you. You stand over there, against that wall. Open your mouth wide and I'll run and jump down your throat."

So the wolf stood with his mouth well open. The ram went back, lowered his head, took a good run, and butted the wolf as hard as he could straight in the mouth, knocking out most of his other teeth. Then he went away.

After a moment or two the wolf picked himself up, feeling rather giddy. Then he said, "Did I eat him? Or didn't I? I *think* I did."

Antosia, blinking, dazed, whispering to herself in the wolf's voice, pleased the audience nearly as much as she had Bobby White. "Encore!" they shouted, though they knew very well there were to be no encores. Tossie made them a polite curtsey, and then beckoned to Judy who, most surprisingly, turned around and produced a pipe. No one had ever suspected her of such a thing. Antosia, however, had wormed it out of her at once. She had joined a Pipers' Guild class when she was convalescent, made a pipe and learned to play it. Now here she was, playing a curious tune that went up and then down and then up again, a bugle-call of a tune that half announced something and then suddenly stopped, broke off. Now what was Antosia after? This was something quite different. She was looking so serious too, all forehead and big eyes, with her hair thrown back like that.

"Now," said Antosia gravely, "now you are in the watch-
man's chamber in the spire of the Church of Our Lady in
Krakow. You have heard the watchman calling the hour on
his trumpet. He did not finish it—he can never finish it.
Always he must break off like that, a shot bird. I will tell
you why. When the Tartar armies came rushing across
Poland, like a great dark wave, they reached the walls of
Krakow and came bursting into the streets. The watchman
in his spire seized his trumpet to arouse the city. The
Tartars drew their bows to kill him. They shot. An arrow
pierced his throat—" Antosia's hands clasped her neck, her
voice quivered and dropped, she looked agonized. "He fell
as he played. And so he died. But we never forget him. Ever
since then the watchman plays his trumpet like that—
breaking off . . . dying. And Krakow remembers—the
Tartars have been gone for centuries, but Krakow remembers." (The way Antosia said those words, "Krakow remembers," set your eyes pricking—you couldn't help it, as
Bridget told Grannie afterwards. And that was perfectly
true about the trumpet tune. The watchman still plays
it like that, or did until the Germans came, never finish-
ing; and then he hits a bell with a hammer, and he's frightfully unpunctual, you can't go by him at all, but that
doesn't matter. You never hear him without thinking of
the arrow, if you're Tossie.)

The audience stirred and sighed and blew their noses,
partly for the story and partly for Antosia's face; then she
turned funny again. They finished up their twenty minutes
of Poland with Krak, the Hooded Knight, who slew his
Dragon, not with his lance as did St. George but with a
dead sheep stuffed full of sulphur. The Dragon ate it and

was smitten with such a thirst that it drank the Vistula River right up and burst, and so died. Antosia was the sheep and Remove strung themselves into a white dragon, tied up in sheets in some wonderful way, and ate her. The reptile roared and drank, making squelching noises, drank again, and finally died with Rosemary Parke (and who would have thought she could act?) as Krak, watching the death throes; and then the Dragon surprised them by reviving, to dance off through the audience and out of the gallery, the sheep after it, with Krak and Judy to sing its dancing tune. A great windup.

There was no question about it. Judges and audience were agreed. Amid storms of applause, Remove took its place beside the Sixth as the chosen entertainers for the party.

> 5 <

Grannie and Bridget walked home arm-in-arm after the show—or, rather, Grannie walked and Bridget pranced beside her, so overjoyed was she at the way it had gone.

"Gosh, Tossie was marvelous! She was a success, a real howling success, wasn't she!"

"She was indeed."

"How she got that old Remove of hers so keen about Poland—that's what beats me. They'd hardly heard of the place—where that war started, that's about all they knew—and now they're mad about it. Bats, absolutely, like she is. They're all over the place, singing about the Orava Road and their hoofs resounding and their chestnuts bounding—Violet thought it meant chestnuts roasting and hopping out of the fire when they're done. Silly thing!"

"Not really like Antosia, though," said Grannie.

Bridget stopped prancing and walked soberly for a few steps to consider this. After a moment she agreed.

"No, not really. No one could be like Tossie when it comes to Poland."

Tossie at her prie-Dieu—she was a Roman Catholic so she said special prayers in Polish that Bridget did not understand—praying, Bridget knew, for Poland; Tossie persuading the music mistresses to play Chopin, listening as no one else listened, not just with her ears but with her whole self; Tossie's face when she seized a newspaper—a thing Bridget herself seldom did—and went off into the corner with it; no, Tossie never forgot Poland, from one end of the day to the other. No one else could possibly be like that.

"Hm," murmured Grannie thoughtfully. "It's difficult for you English children, taking your country for granted as we all do, to understand what Antosia feels for hers. More than difficult; impossible."

Bridget was ready to argue that.

"I understand a good bit. I make a pretty good shot at it, anyway."

Nevertheless Bridget began to see the sense of that "Impossible" when Antosia came in that night. Both she and Grannie had gone to bed, but she jumped up and hung over the banisters, James beside her, to shout, "Hallo, Tossie, come and tell us the news." The Sixth had given a supper party for themselves and Remove to wind up the day and Bridget was dying to hear about it; also to pass on some of the congratulations and nice remarks she had picked up.

Antosia called out something unintelligible about there being no hurry.

Buried in Grannie's big chair

"Now then, don't you go giving yourself airs, Queen of the Remove, or I'll set Mrs. Drake on you again. You come up or I'll come and fetch you."

But Antosia wasn't giving herself airs or anything like it. She couldn't speak. She was in the sitting room, buried in Grannie's big chair, her head on its arm, her face hidden in her white sleeves, her skirt with all the orange, red, blue, yellow stripes flowing round her like the fruitful plains of her country, her body shaking with little choked sobs, the most difficult, bitter crying Bridget had ever heard.

"*Tossie!* What's the matter? I thought you'd be feeling glorious. You're tired, you're half dead. And it all went so beautifully—far better than ever before. Addy said to Grannie that you couldn't only act and dance yourself but that you made other people—"

But it didn't matter what even Miss Adams had said. Antosia only sobbed on into her white sleeve without raising her head; and Bridget knew she had gone away into her own enormous private grief where no one could follow her —grief for her country.

She went into the kitchen and brewed some chocolate, the most comforting thing she could think of. By the time she had done that and hunted up the biscuits Antosia was recovering—that was one of the blessed things about her; she recovered from her fits of rage, grief, curiosity, frantic impatience, quicker than anyone in the world. She was right way up in the chair, looking rather white, but without that blotched look that most people get if they so much as shed a tear. Her eyes were a bit red but her nose wasn't. "Great grandmother Bridget," she murmured, but she drank her chocolate and ate her biscuit. Then she flung back her curtain of hair, put her head up, and said, "I'm a coward. Krak's always telling me I'm a coward."

"Coward? And you doing the matador for Mrs. Drake's bull. Bunk."

Antosia brushed that aside.

"The bull was nothing—there was no time to be afraid. I used to say I would never live on an island—always I should be afraid of falling off into the sea and I hate the sea. But when I see you all, so sure, so secure on your British island, so happy and making plans—" She stopped —then threw up her head again. "But in our song we sing, 'Poland is not dead for we still live.'"

"Live? I should just think you did live," said Bridget, encouraging this new spirit. "It'd take more than an old war to stop you being alive and kicking."

"I'll sing that song to you—"

"No, don't. Not now. Have another biscuit. What were
the Sixth like? Snooty? I bet you talked so much you
didn't eat a thing. I bet you're ravenous."

"Yes, I am—ravenous. A great fierce word, ravenous . . .
like wolves coming out of the forest across the snow."

Her eyes took a sudden glint and the ring was coming
back to her voice. All the same, it wouldn't do. They'd
had enough of Poland. Better give it a rest, snow and songs
and all, thought Bridget.

"Blow the wolves. Give James a biscuit—he's ravenous,
too. Then we'd better go to bed; it's pretty late and we'll
keep Grannie awake."

Grannie was awake all right. On Bridget's dressing table
was a bottle of aspirin and a note—"If you think it advis-
able, give Antosia one of these." Now wasn't that like
Grannie? never fussing, leaving them alone, though she
must have heard them; leaving her to manage Tossie,
even to decide whether she should or should not have
aspirin. Grannie believed in leaving people alone to look
after their own affairs.

And she could manage Antosia. She waited a little; then
crept into her room to see if she was asleep. She was;
lying flat on her face, her hair streaming over the pillow,
her clothes in a ring on the floor where she had dropped
them off like some bright animal shedding its skin—awful,
the way she *would* do that. Bridget tidied up by the dusky
light of evening slowly turning to night, put the Polish
dress away—no more Poland with exams beginning tomorrow—and laid out the Ramparts uniform. There wasn't
a great deal you could do for Tossie, so much of her was
out of reach, she went away into worlds where you couldn't
follow her; but here was something. Ramparts would be the

first thing she thought of tomorrow when her eye lit on that uniform, not Poland.

⊁ 6 ⊰

But term hadn't quite done with them. It still had a last kick in it and a pretty startling one, like the last bang of a squib.

They never did any work on the last day, they collected their things, began their good-byes, and sat about and talked till break, when the exam results and the new forms for next term were posted up. Bridget had hardly been at Ramparts an hour when Miss Adams sent for her.

"Gosh, what've I done?" she quavered.

The Sixth who brought the message was kind.

"Nothing, probably. You're not sent up. She's in Paradise—she does that sometimes. Hurry up."

Bridget took her way soberly down the corridor. What ages it seemed since she had followed Tossie skipping down it in her air-borne suit and seen her knock as casually as if it was the door of Grannie's bedroom at Green Hedges! She wouldn't behave like that now, she'd know better; but the chances were she'd say, "Look at me, the British schoolgirl," taking off one of them, walk, manner, voice, and everything else, so that they knew exactly which it was. She could and did mimic them all.

Bridget knocked her discreet Lower Fourth knock and walked into Paradise. It was looking different; a July room now, roses in the copper jug instead of chrysanthemums, no fire, but a summer sun pouring in. Addy, however, remained the same.

"Come in, Bridget. Have some cherries and sit down. I

want to talk to you."

Heavens, what about? Bridget took a very small cherry. No good choking instead of answering up properly if Addy started on questions.

"You've done well in exams, you know," Miss Adams began blandly. "You've got a good sound brain, inherited from your father no doubt, so you needn't trouble to deny it, and your grandmother must be a better teacher than most of us. You've more than caught up with your form, torpedo and all."

There was no answer to that and anyway, Bridget's jaws were frozen with surprise. Done *well?* Gosh! But what was it all leading up to?

"I'm proposing therefore to give you a double remove."

"But—" Bridget swallowed the cherry "what into?" Remove? Glorious, heavenly to be in Tossie's form, but *not* Remove, not with all the freaks and duds and geniuses—

"Into the Lower Fifth," continued Addy's cool voice. "What I'm wondering is whether or not to put Antosia into the same form."

Bridget collected her wits. This was like that first talk; it was going to take some managing. Well, she'd got Antosia into Ramparts that time, why shouldn't she get her into the Lower Fifth this?

"She's good enough in some subjects for the Upper Fifth and she's bad enough in others for the Third. We can manage that, of course. Nevertheless . . ."

That awful word. People stayed in Remove, traveling about into different sets and forms for the things they were good at for half their school life. Or so people said. And fairly fed up they were, too.

And then, surprisingly, Addy asked, "What do you think yourself?"

"Well . . . of course I want her frightfully." It seemed better to be honest about it.

"So I imagined. Back in the same boat again." Miss Adams smiled. "Nevertheless . . ." She stopped.

You couldn't very well say, "Well, what?" so Bridget took another cherry and waited.

"If you two are going to have one of these very exclusive friendships, the kind that keep other people, other things, other ideas out, I'd better leave her where she is; you'd be bad for each other and a nuisance in the form. If, on the other hand, you're going to pull your weight together—I don't seem able to get away from that boat, do I?—do whatever's going, get to know everyone and don't spend all the time sitting in each other's pockets, you might be quite a help. I'm rather wondering which sort of friendship it's going to be." And she looked at Bridget as if she really was wondering.

No good vaguely making promises; they'd cut no ice with Addy. She knew exactly what she meant. There were a lot of these couples mooning about, no good to anyone but themselves. Tossie mimicked them and laughed at them and called them the Gooseberry Fools, rubbed through a sieve, so mingled that you didn't know which was which. Bridget took another cherry while her wits raced around, looking for something to say, some nice hard, convincing facts to show she and Tossie would never be like that.

"As a matter of fact," she managed finally, "Antosia has a lot of friends already that I hardly know at all. Elspeth MacDonald came to tea and talked Scotland and Poland with her and Grannie, and I didn't understand a word. And Judy comes and plays and I don't like it a bit. And then there was their Polish show, I didn't know a word about it till I saw it. She never told me a thing. We don't sit in each other's pockets at Green Hedges, there's too much to do. Besides, Antosia's really much too clever. She doesn't sit anywhere much."

"True, she doesn't. She's bursting out of Remove. I'm disbanding it—" Miss Adams stopped. Bridget held her breath. Was there a "nevertheless" coming? "A bigger form is a necessity for her. Judy and Elspeth, Rosemary Parke and Antoinette will be going into the Lower Fifth, too." She paused. No "nevertheless" and Bridget sighed with relief.

"A very interesting lot," she quoted from Grannie, to fill in.

"Yes, very," said Miss Adams absent-mindedly. "But not easy." She woke up and became very brisk. "Here, what am I doing, discussing all these things with you? You're full of sense, Bridget. For goodness' sake, help us all by using it. We make school friends that last us a lifetime— why not? There is no place where we know each other better. There's a lot you and Antosia can do for each other, but remember there's a lot more the pair of you can do for others. That's what I wanted to say. The lists will be up at break. Don't tell Antosia or anyone until then. That's all. Thank you."

Bridget walked thoughtfully down the corridor. They were good cherries, but she hardly knew there was still one in her mouth until she almost swallowed it, stone and all.

SCAURBANK

Chapter VI

> 1 <

ADDY needn't have worried, Bridget said to herself. Once in the Fifth, a big form, she and Antosia seemed to see nothing of each other. They were both in the hockey eleven, but Bridget was almost at once given a place in the Ramparts' Second eleven—centre half, what was more —and that put her into different and more superior games at different times.

"I wish you were in it, too," she said to Tossie. "You could be, I'm sure, if you swatted at it. You're frightfully fast, they all say so."

But Antosia only said briskly, "Next year I will—what d'you call it?—swat. This year, no," and proceeded to start a form dramatic club. In the Fifth you could do things like that; that was one of the blessings of having skipped the Upper Fourth, where you couldn't.

The whole form wanted to belong, they stood round her insisting on it; but she was very decided about who she would and would not have, very severe in fact.

"The limitation—" she said, her English becoming a little strange, as it always did when she was cornered, "the limitation will be ten. There will be in the club only those of talent. No dud nor freak—" She was pleased with those two words, but she had very little idea what they meant. "There will be Judy to play the piano and her pipe —but she must learn the dance tunes on it. There will be Toinette because she is gay and she can sing. Elspeth, who can teach us her Scottish dances, and I will have Rosemary because she is solemn and funny—to be funny and not laugh yourself is to be much funnier. The rest—" and she explained a most severe competitive test. Not only had the members to be able to dance and sing and act but they had to promise certain times for rehearsing, and they had to take a vow of secrecy. "Surprise—" said Antosia, and reeled off Miss Adams's famous remark about its being drama's greatest aid.

"How they stand you, Antosia, I can't think," said Grannie, when she heard this. "A new girl, and a Pole into the bargain."

"But I'm good. They know I'm good," said Antosia calmly. "I can think of ways for them to act, things they can do, and I can make them do it."

And she could, as Bridget explained afterwards. "If a person is frightfully confident like that when they *can't* do a thing, then it's conceit—they blow up like a balloon and get pricked and that's the end of them. But if they're confident and they *can* do it, then it's just sensible."

"I see," said Grannie. " 'He who knows, and knows that he knows, is wise. Follow him.' "

"Yes, that's it exactly. I didn't try for the club because I want to play all the hockey I possibly can, but I don't

believe I'd have got in if I had." And she said to herself,
"Addy can put that in her pipe and smoke it."

The term flew. Antosia's club gave a performance to the
rest of the school for break-up which was quite a success,
if not the sensation of the Polish affair. The center half of
the first eleven went down with a fearful cold the day of an
important match and Bridget took her place, with Grannie
on the touch line, following her every movement.

"You must hit *harder*, much harder," she said afterwards, and took her out into the garden again to practice,
but she acknowledged that it was a sound performance.

"It is as if you played at a concert," said Tossie, much
amused. "Grannie is a wonderful audience. I shall make
her come to my tennis in the summer."

Holidays flew, too. Antosia danced and sang in her
Polish dress at a party Grannie gave for the Women's In-
stitute, and Mrs. Drake, who belonged but never went to
meetings, actually not only attended but arrived half an
hour early to tell them all about Tossie and the bull. What
between that and her gay dress and her funny stories Tossie had a great reception.

"Oh, I'm happy, I'm happy, I'm happy!" she cried, and
danced home ahead of them in the soft dark of the
January evening, out of sight, though not out of hearing.
"Grannie and Green Hedges, Ramparts and my club,
Bridget and her hockey . . ."

That was one of Antosia's charms, Grannie said; when
she was happy she said so, she took nothing for granted.
"She's never sure how long anything will last, so she makes
the very most of it—I suppose that's it."

"But Ramparts and Green Hedges *will* last," argued
Bridget.

"Perhaps. But who knows if Antosia will last with them. What if that father turns up?—as let's hope he will."

"She never hears from him."

"No one hears much of Poles unless they're in this country. And there's Uncle Krak."

"She hasn't heard from him either."

"But she certainly will."

And there Grannie was right; she did. She had a letter from him just as the Easter term began. He was going somewhere on a special mission. He would be back in the summer and would try to get leave and see her. The letter was of course in Polish so there was no question of handing it over to Grannie or reading it aloud or anything like that. All the same, Tossie might have been a little more forthcoming about it, Bridget thought.

"Is that all? Just that he's going away?"

"Yes, that's all—" and there was Tossie with that curious withdrawn look that meant "Poland." Bridget had hardly seen that look since the evening of the party when she had come home half-dead and been revived with hot chocolate. "He also says he thinks my father is well. He doesn't know, but he thinks."

"*Thinks?* But where is your father, child?" Grannie looked up from her own letters. It was the last day of the holidays and they were all having nine o'clock breakfast together.

"In Poland. Warsaw, perhaps."

"Heavens, that dangerous place? What's he doing there?"

Antosia shrugged her shoulders, as who should say, "Nobody knows."

"Oh, come on, Tossie, what else did Uncle Krak say?

When's he coming here?" Bridget was feeling irritated, disturbed.

"When he comes back."

"What sort of a mission is it? Where?"

"That he does not say. It is all very security."

"Secret, you mean, dear," murmured Grannie.

"He calls it 'security' in English. That means, I think, a war meaning, very extra secret. I must guess, he says."

"And can you?" asked Bridget.

"Yes."

She dropped the little word out very gently; it was like the small *plop* of a pebble dropped into a pond, making quiet rings in the silence it caused. The mission was to Poland, of course; it would be fearfully exciting to know how he got there and what he had to do, and there was Tossie, every door slammed, locked and double-locked and that "security" look on guard.

"Three pages black with writing just to say that?" grumbled Bridget.

"Ah, that—that is to tell me what *I* must do."

"You?" Bridget opened her eyes wide at that. "But what have you got to do, except get on with everything at Ramparts? Isn't that enough?"

"Enough?" Antosia laughed a little wildly and got up—putting her letter very carefully inside her jumper, though, as Bridget observed. "It is enough and too much. We go back tomorrow and have I not seven more sums to do? Yes, yes, yes, I have."

"Then settle down and do them," advised Grannie, and gathered up her letters. "This is our last lazy morning. It's wet and you'd better get down to it and not be lazy any more. Bridget will help you."

≻ 2 ≺

Summer came, Antosia threw her dramatic club overboard and plunged into tennis. There was a convenient wall
that ran alongside the lawn of Green Hedges and she was
to be heard every morning at half past six, hitting her ball
against it, backhand, forehand, backhand, forehand. Nothing surprising in that—when Tossie was keen on a thing
she was very keen—but what was astonishing was the fact
that you could set your clock by her. Tossie, who had no
idea of time! James, in his basket, gave a sleepy yap when
he heard her and Bridget turned over as if a clock had
struck, knowing she had another half hour.

"Time is a thing Krak says I must have," said Antosia,
when Bridget marveled at her. "Punctuality, he says, is
security. You meet a person at seven minutes past one and
it must *be* seven minutes past one, not earlier or later. I
must learn time, he says; also to win at tennis, no matter
what the handicap."

So she was no longer late for everything; but she didn't
win the American tournament because the games mistress,
who did the handicapping, saw to it that she didn't—what
was the good of Antosia, she said, if she couldn't take defeat? Poor Tossie, scarlet in the face, rushed about the
court, trying for everything, searching for her opponent's
weak spot, working for her own best stroke, never forgetting the score for a moment; and minding, minding ter-
ribly, when she was beaten.

"But what does it matter, Tossie?" Bridget would argue.
"That girl's in the Sixth, you couldn't possibly give her
half thirty. You did very well to get three games out of

her. After all, you got the whole of the eight out of Elspeth and she's supposed to be rather good. I thought she was going to die of surprise."

"She was not a strong enemy."

"*Enemy?*" Bridget laughed. "What words you use!"

"But when you play, it is an enemy you defeat. You must hate her."

"Bunk. Nothing would make you hate Elspeth."

"I love her—but when I must win, I hate her."

"Right-o, have it your own way. Grind your teeth and hiss if you like. Fee-fo-fum, I smell the blood of an English wo-man. You've got Violet to play next and she'll probably cry at the sight of you. I say, d'you know you're being put into the Six. You're going to be told today. The Form are frightfully pleased."

"*No!* Never! Am I? Oh, Bridget . . ."

Enemies forgotten, Antosia burst into *See my chestnut bounding,* danced across the court, flung her racquet away, leaped the net to get it, and danced back again.

"Here, hold on, that's my racquet," shouted Bridget, but it made no difference. They both knew it was hers, Tossie always took it when she had a match to play—hadn't Krak told her she had to win?

"You needn't go chucking it about," said Bridget, as grumpily as she could. "And I was hunting for it all over the place. I've got to play myself in a minute."

"No, I needn't take it, but I do," cried Antosia, still in an ecstasy. "And I must chuck everything about, I'm so happy. Come and see when the next match is." She seized Bridget's hand with her warm, quicksilver one, and rushed her to the board. "Quite soon. Next week. Who will be my partner? Grannie must come." But when the

Head of Games came up to tell her the good news she behaved beautifully.

"I was calm. I said 'thank you' as if I did not care at all.
I was English. I was almost like Bridget," she told Grannie
that night, "but all the time I was singing like a lark inside. 'Now I play for the honor of Ramparts,' I sang.
Hola-too-ra-loo—"

"All right, child, I'm delighted," said Grannie, "only
don't set James off barking. He never seems able to stop."
For Antosia was no longer singing inside but out loud in
Polish, in a voice that filled Green Hedges. "I think it's
time you had singing lessons with that voice of yours. How
old are you? I've forgotten."

"Fourteen."

"Too young. You ought to be seventeen."

"*Seventeen?*" Antosia's face changed, one of those swift
alterations that turned her in a moment into someone entirely different. "Oh, where shall I be when I'm seventeen?"

> 3 <

They had spent the Easter holidays planting potatoes
for a farmer near by. How should they spend the long,
precious summer holidays?

"You must do war work, of course," said Grannie, "but
you'd be better for a change, too. I shall ask Mrs. Drake
about that farmer brother of hers in Cumberland, whether
you could board with them and work. All farmers want
help at harvest time and you're a couple of strong girls
who could do a lot. How would you like that?"

"We'd love it," said Bridget at once. "James, too?"

"I expect so. One dog more or less doesn't make much

difference, and he's not a fighter, thank goodness."

Antosia was enchanted at the idea. In Poland, she told them, summer holidays were huge—and she stretched her arms wide to show them how huge. The schools, in fact, only did a half-day's work for most of the summer, but they sometimes worked all night long in the fields.

"But they couldn't see."

"Yes, they can. Nights are short and there is moonlight and it's cool. Oh, but it is hot in the sun! The land bakes and you bake with it. You touch the corn and it's hot. Oh, I shall like to feel that again, that hot straw. We have big hats, do we?"

"Mackintoshes and rubber boots, more likely," said Grannie, "and they're precious hard to get. It's lucky I've got some to lend you."

She packed the two girls off in the middle of August for a month while she herself paid some visits and Drake and Mrs. Drake did some cleaning up in the house and garden.

Bridget and Antosia did their best to dig information out of Mrs. Drake as to where they were going and what it would be like. The brother was called Firbeck, Alan Firbeck, and he had a farm on the river side, not far from the great road up which runaway couples had once galloped to the smithy at Gretna Green to get married.

"Is it a big farm, Mrs. Drake?"

"Big enough. His father had it before him. Scaurbank, it is. Ye'll see the room where I was born—the bed, likely enough. Alan was never one for changes."

Gosh, was all Bridget could say to that.

"Then it is very old," said Antosia briskly. "I like houses

to be old and small like they are in England. Animals?
Cattle, are there?"

"Alan's got a good herd of Frisians and he's doing well
with pigs, he says."

"We go up into the mountains with our cattle in Poland;
there's good grazing up there. Are there mountains?"

"Not at Scaurbank. Ye'll see Skiddaw standing one way
and the Scottish hills the other, but where you're going
it's as flat as my hand, with a river running away outside
the door."

"Rivers. I love rivers," said Antosia dreamily, "rushing
rivers when the snow melts and the ice cracks—"

"You don't get it frozen over, not once in forty years,"
said Mrs. Drake practically. "Flows up half the time, not
down, with the tide—"

"Tide?" Antosia's voice suddenly sharpened. "That
sounds like the sea."

"So it is, too. Sea's a couple of miles away."

"Oh, Bridget, *not* the sea! I can't go to the sea. I hate
it. I hate boats. I hate the gobbling and chuckling. I hate
the waves—I can't—" she seized Bridget by the arm, suddenly distracted.

"Keep your hair on and don't *fuss*," said Bridget—you
had to be rather stolid when Tossie turned like this. "Who
said waves? It's an estuary—sand flats, marsh, heaps of
birds, Grannie says. We're going to work on the *land*, you
don't go harvesting in the sea. You needn't go near a boat
if you don't want to."

"But tides mean sea—"

"A big tide's a bonny sight," said Mrs. Drake almost
tenderly, as she remembered it. "Covers the sands and the
marsh right over—"

She was now cramming on the felt hat

"There—like a lake," put in Bridget hastily.

"A lake—yes, I can love a lake, quiet and still water, but a tide—"

Mrs. Drake went on, hearing nothing. "—right over, it does. And when the wind's behind it and the bore comes up—"

"Oh, what's a bore?"

But Mrs. Drake had reminisced enough. That bull had put three minutes on to her journey to Green Hedges every time she took it, going round by the road as she did, and she'd be in a hurry for the rest of her days. She was now cramming on the felt hat that had replaced the straw with the violets. "You'll soon see. Now I'm away. I've me work to do and I can't waste more of me time chattering. You'll have your work to do too, at Scaurbank, if my niece Maggie's after you. She's a grand girl to work, they say, but, my word—" and Mrs. Drake was gone.

> 4 <

Scaurbank, Mr. Firbeck, Ronnie Firbeck, Blades and Mrs. Blades from the long, low, white cottage by the road, and Maggie; and *Maggie*. How interesting it was to come to a new place, to meet a different lot of people, to have quite another kind of life, to spend the day doing things like standing up sheaves of corn, eight together, so that they didn't fall down. How *very* interesting. And what glorious weather they had brought. Bridget looked at her brown arm, burned a most satisfactory tan, as she lay in bed for ten minutes' wakefulness before sleep. James was flat on the floor, sleeping and kicking and giving an occasional hunting whimper; James was enjoying himself at Scaurbank. Tossie across the room was off already. She fell asleep quicker and woke more slowly than anyone else in the world.

They had been at Scaurbank a week; quarter of the precious month had gone. It seemed a shame to sleep away more of it than you could possibly help and Bridget got up quietly to lean out of the open window and take a last look at the river. Everyone was in bed: even Maggie was asleep, probably kicking and murmuring like James, chasing the work she pursued all day and never caught up with, even in her dreams.

Dead low tide. The red of the sunset had faded out and a light mist was coming up, washing everything in silver. The swans down there looked as if they were staying the night. Bridget counted them—eighteen. They were wild-tame swans, Ronnie had told her, the young ones, the boys and girls who spend the first seven years of their lives enjoying themselves together before settling down to eggs and cygnets and responsible life. This time of year they came most evenings, fishing, preening themselves, swimming lazily, just enough to keep their places against the current. Bridget never looked at them without thinking of the princes in the fairy story who were changed into swans until such time as the magic shirts were woven that changed them back again. But one shirt had no sleeve and the youngest prince kept his wing as a man—and a very nice thing to have, thought Bridget, as a swan stood in the shallows and lazily flapped. Did they have sentinels to keep watch, like wild geese? There were two floating by themselves on either side of the group, one facing upstream and one down; so perhaps they did. She must ask Ronnie; he didn't mind what you asked him.

The swans fished and preened themselves. One or two waddled, waddled hideously—oh, they should never be allowed to land—ashore. Others edged to the shallows and folded their long necks into their wings in some miraculous way, and slept. Bridget yawned. In another minute she would tear herself away and sleep, too; as soon as the swans dimmed to nothing; as soon as they were just a handful of goose feathers blown on to the water. It was going to be hot again tomorrow. She'd bathe on that nice little bit of sand where it was deep enough at high tide. But was it really true that in another fortnight or so the sea would come up and, if there was a wind, cover sands, banks, marsh and all? Ronnie said so, and he knew. Once, he said, a Scottish army had come marauding down over the Border when there was no border. They'd crossed the marsh easy enough, but there was no getting back. The tide came up with a great wind behind it and lo! there they were in the sea, and that was the end of them. Not a man got home to Scotland.

Oh, well, nothing fierce like that happened nowadays. Good-bye, swans; have a nice party and come again to-morrow. Good fishing and happy dreams. Bridget waved her hand to them, and in five minutes she was asleep and dreaming herself.

➤ 5 ◄

She woke as usual to the sound of Maggie's clogs in the yard below her window. She and Antosia wore clogs, too, but hers were green and Tossie's were scarlet, whereas Maggie's were a dour black, well greased and seldom cleaned. You could tell they were workaday shoes by the very sound of them, Bridget thought, as she listened to their quick click-clop.

Maggie would have been on the run since half past five, lighting the fire, getting the kettle to boil, preparing the seven o'clock breakfast for her uncle and Ronnie, weaving in and out of the rooms and the yard, her body slanting as she took the corners with the pace she went. It seemed awful to Bridget that she should work so hard.

"But *must* you get up at half past five, Maggie?"

"Aye," said Maggie, who had no time to spend on super-fluous words. Couldn't they lay breakfast overnight and save time that way? Bridget had asked, but Maggie had been scandalized at the very idea of such slovenly ways.

"I don't see why it's slovenly," Bridget argued.

"My cleaning."

"You could do that after breakfast, couldn't you?"

"Hens."

"Couldn't the hens wait?"

But the look in Maggie's eye as she ran from the room told how little the hens could wait, or the pigs who came after and had to have their potatoes boiled and the pig-bucket emptied, and that awful stuff that was left when the butter was made, fetched. And on the heels of that came the special work of the day; washing on Monday, cleaning the house on Tuesday, butter and cheese making (Maggie made a wonderful cream cheese) on Wednesday, baking on Thursday, market on Friday, and then Saturday, a frenzy of getting everything ready for Sunday. And people forever being fed; there was the ten o'clock snack, the twelve o'clock dinner, the three o'clock tea, and the seven o'clock tea, and the nightcap of a supper before bed.

"It's no good, Bridget," said Antosia, amused at Bridget's face as she went through this appalling timetable, "Maggie must run. 'See how they run' you say in your funny song, but I think it is not the mice who run but the farmer's wife."

"As if she had a carving knife after her, too," agreed Bridget ruefully. "And when she has sitting hens it's much worse, she says. The geese don't even turn their eggs over for themselves, she has to do it for them every morning, and they all have to be put to bed and got up, and the cows have calves, and the pigs, little pigs."

"Yes," agreed Antosia, who knew something about farms. "In the spring she must have to flash about like lightning."

"But she hasn't time to take her curlers out even now."

But on Friday, market day, out they came. On that day Maggie left a stew on the hob and a bread pudding in the oven, put on her smart green coat, tied a green bandeau round her head, took a large basket and three string bags, and ran off on her good high-heeled shoes that shone like two chestnuts to catch the nine-thirty bus for a half-hour ride into the town. It was a wonder, Antosia said, that she could sit still for so long, a wonder that she didn't jump out and run alongside from sheer hurry.

It was market day today; the clacking wooden soles below had a brisk, anticipatory sound.

"Wake up, Tossie; Maggie has to get off early."

Antosia wriggled, groaned, stretched, groaned again and at last sat up blinking.

"Now don't you go saying 'Where am I?' like a person in a book."

"I won't, because I know. I'm in heaven—Scaurbank. But it's not seven. I'm asleep."

"Yes, it is. And Maggie wants us early."

Grannie had arranged that the girls should not get up earlier than seven. By the time they came down to breakfast the men had gone out and their bacon and fried eggs sat between two plates on the top of the stove, their tea beside it.

"Why?"

"Market day."

"*See how she runs, see how she runs,*" chanted Antosia. "That, I think, must be the national song of your British women—"

But Bridget wasn't listening, she was at the window. Nine of the swans were still there. Oh, if she could have seen the others go—a few flaps of their great wings on the water and then a straight sailing up into the sky, all nine of them.

"I shall stand up the sheaves all the morning and then

Ronnie says it will be done. What shall we do then?"

Bridget turned round.

"I shall bathe."

"Oh, no, no, *no!*" Antosia dived under the bedclothes again and became a muffled voice, groaning out volleys of noes.

"I shall. Preen and bathe and sit about and bathe again, like the swans. You needn't. You can sit in the sun and chew a bit of straw with your back to me. Or read. And I shall mess about with the boat—"

"No, no, *no!*" came again, louder.

"I shall. I'm going over to the other side of the river."

Antosia's head came out.

"But can you?"

"Yes. It used to be a ferry, Ronnie says. There's a little sort of pier thing the other side. You needn't even get your feet wet if you come."

"Hm. I'd rather like to go to the other side."

"Well, then, come along. I told you it was no good saying you'd never get into a boat again; you'll have to. Everyone in England gets into a boat sooner or later, so you may as well begin today."

"No. No boats, please, Grandmother."

"Then I'll go across alone and see where I get, and I'll take a basket for mushrooms. Ronnie says sometimes the whole marsh is covered with them. You can peel them when I come back."

But the day didn't work out like that.

The last of the wheat was cut and the sheaves stood up into stooks, that field was done; but Firbeck decided to start on his barley. They'd brought the right weather with them, these two, he said, and he'd make the most of it for fear they took it away again. The glass was still high but it was inclined to fall. Could they come along out as soon as might be after dinner? Of course they would, said Bridget, but she thought she'd just wash up the dinner things first. Antosia would go along with them and she would follow.

And that was how it came to be that she was alone at Scaurbank when Uncle Krak walked in.

UNCLE KRAK

R. GERVIS

Chapter VII

> 1 <

HE looked magnificent in his battle dress—as if hewn out
of bronze, Bridget thought. His face, very grim and strong
with its big nose and closely shut lips, was bronzed and
shining with sweat this hot day; his plum-colored beret
was off and his hair was long enough to go into hard, wet-
looking ripples like a statue's. It was as if an effigy out of a
cathedral had opened the door and strode into the scullery.

"*Uncle Krak!*" she cried (Uncle George as a name didn't
suit him any more), holding up her dripping plate, staring
at his face that seemed so much older than she remembered—and then she made the stupidest remark that ever
was. "You've grown!"

His statue face cracked into a laugh and suddenly he was
young again, the boy who had waved to them like a mad-
man on the pier.

"But you haven't said 'Hallo.' You always say 'Hallo.'
If I met you in the streets of heaven or if I dropped down
beside you with my parachute, you would say 'Hallo.'
Say it."

"Hallo, then. And have you dropped?"

No, he hadn't. Grannie had told him where they were and he'd come by train and bus and on his feet, and he had ten days' leave which he proposed to spend with them.

"Oh, how lovely! But—"

Bridget faltered. How was Maggie going to take this? Where would he sleep? There was no room for him. They made a lot of extra work as it was, she said; how could she bear to have still one more? And what would Mr. Firbeck say? And Ronnie? Oh, how frightfully suddenly Poles did things!

Krak was smiling at her, understanding exactly.

"I shall sleep anywhere, in the hay, or, better, on the straw out there. I shall eat anything. I shall want no hot water, for I shall swim in the river. I talk English better, very well now. I find the British always very kind."

"Oh, they are kind, the Firbecks are angels—they'll be delighted. And it'll be heavenly having you—Tossie will die of joy when she sees you." Bridget piled it on, all she knew, for fear he should think he was not wanted. All the same, there was Maggie. Wouldn't it be the last straw, a good big heavy one, too? And what happened when the camel's back broke?

"I tell you what, Krak. Maggie, who runs this house and works like a slave and an ant and a beaver all in one, is just coming back by bus. Let's go and meet her and say you've come."

"Now, you mean?"

"Yes, now. I'll put these dishes away. You drop that thing off your back and we'll go along."

Maggie staggered out of the bus hung with bursting bags and parcels like a Christmas tree. She had brought their

Bursting with bags and parcels like a Christmas tree

week's rations—heavy enough, goodness knows—and besides that, a dead weight of fresh herrings that had turned up unexpectedly in the town, some of their points spent on tins of beans, vegetables—Scaurbank had no garden—a new tin bucket and a large flat enamel bowl. Surely even Maggie couldn't have carried it all. Bridget introduced Krak as quickly as she could. He made his best foreign bow, took the basket in one hand and all three string bags in the other—with this weight, he said, he'd need a drop of a mile at least. They'd carried ninety pounds, he'd been

told, the British soldiers of the last war, and the Land
Army seemed to be carrying it still. He filled the basin with
cauliflowers and gave it to Bridget as her share, and there
was Maggie with just the bucket and the carrots—a mere
nothing. All this was so satisfactory that the moment they
were fairly started Bridget put in her word.

"Antosia's uncle has ten days' leave."

Maggie stopped dead. "Eh, but where's the bed for
him?" The Scaurbank hunting look returned and she
started off at a run.

"No bed wanted. I've brought my rations—"

"There's plenty—plenty butter, plenty milk, plenty
cheese, eggs—there's a couple o' cockerel—" Maggie was
flying along, her mind already darting about the larder at
home. "Sofa's hard, but likely you'll—"

"He rather likes sleeping just anywhere," put in Bridget.
"His lot go in for that kind of thing—"

"I wouldn't like for him not to be comfortable—"

"Perfectly comfortable—" Maggie had now taken to her
heels like the Red Queen in *Alice* and Bridget was running
to keep up.

"If I grow soft on soft beds, they turn me out—pouf—"

"Maggie, what will Mr. Firbeck say?"

"Nowt. Take him out with the three o'clock." And
Maggie shot upstairs like a rocket to get out of her market
clothes.

"It's all right, Krak—" Her "uncle" seemed to have disappeared, like Tossie's. "Maggie's always in a frightful
hurry. They'll love you to stay, I'm sure."

"Stay? There will be no staying," said Krak, as he dis-
entangled himself from all the bags and parcels. "To stay
is to be still. I shall run with Maggie and never be still for

a moment. She will be better than any track work, P.T. exercises, synthetic practice, or anything else. I shall run about after her and carry these enormous weights—she must be made of copper wire and the finest steel—"

"Ssh—she'll be down again in half a second."

She was. The three o'clock tea was on its way to the barley field—even the kettle hurried up its boiling for Maggie—before five minutes had gone. Krak carried the basket so Bridget was free to run on and tell the news.

"Tossie—" she yelled, the wind blowing her voice down to the far corner of the field where Antosio was standing up her stooks. A sheaf in her arm, she looked up.

"*Krak!*" she cried, flung it down, and rushed towards him, arms outstretched, hair flying, her legs taking her leaping and dancing over the stubble.

"Uncle, is it?" said Mr. Firbeck when at last the hugging was over and Tossie had brought the new arrival along. "I don't call to mind my niece Maggie ever ran at me like that."

"He begs to sleep—he hopes to remain—he is in fire to live with us—" Antosia's English slipped and slid as she tried, panting with happiness, to explain.

Everyone laughed. Yes, I'd feel like that, Bridget said to herself, if it was me in Poland, right away from England, and someone of my own came to see me. It was grand to see Tossie bubbling like this. Besides, laughing at her made everyone friends.

Mr. Firbeck shook hands and said, "You're welcome." Ronnie stopped the tractor and came over for his tea and a look at the stranger. Krak got on with them at once. By the time they had finished tea and Bridget was clearing up he was one of the household. He'd take over the trac-

tor, he said, when Ronnie had to go to the milking, meanwhile he'd get on with the stooks, he and Antosia. Bridget
took the basket and started off home. She'd leave them
alone, Tossie and Krak, as much as she could, they'd have
so much to say to each other. Even now she'd heard a
murmur slipped in—"Did you get there, Krak?"—and seen
the nod of the head that answered. So Krak had got to
Poland. How? Goodness knows. Why? Goodness knows.
Tossie must be dying to hear what he'd done, whom he'd
seen. Her aunts in Warsaw? Her father perhaps? Bridget
shook her head. She must be careful not to ask questions,
it was all very "security." Tossie would tell her what she
could, no doubt, in her own time. Meanwhile she'd go
and have a bathe.

The tide was higher, the water a good bit deeper and a
lot colder. She could see now what Ronnie meant about
the current; the bathing wasn't very safe when tides were
higher. There was no question of going across the river as
she had intended. The boat had been drawn up; there it
was, firmly tied to a staple in the yard wall, nowhere near
the water. For the first time since they'd been at Scaurbank, there was no sunset. The sun slipped into a mist and
was lost in a hard dark bank of cloud. There'd be no swans
tonight, a wind had got up that made the river quite rough.

"Goodness, I hope the weather isn't going to break—but
I'm sure it is," Bridget said to herself as she scurried back
to the house. "It's as cold as Christmas." After a fortnight's
gorgeous heat it was quite a shock. She put on a thick
tweed skirt and a woolly and went down to give Maggie
a hand with the supper, looking forward with pleasure to
the warmth of the kitchen.

> 2 <

Bridget was right. He had only one thing against Antosia's uncle, Mr. Firbeck said—he'd broken the weather. It rained all that night and next morning it was raining still. There was nothing much for them to do, so the two girls put on mackintoshes and long boots, tied their heads up in handkerchiefs and took Krak and James for a long walk. Maggie had a message for a farmer two or three miles off and that did for an object. It would have been a nice wet walk, a thing Bridget particularly enjoyed, if it hadn't been for the business of the wire bridge.

A stream that was almost big enough to be called a little river ran behind the farm for which they were bound, on its way to join their big river. Before the war Maggie's friend had gone in for ducks in a big way and their special pond and nesting place had been on the other side of this stream. To get at them he had rigged up a wire bridge, a strand of thick wire rope for the footboard and two thinner ones above to act as balustrades. Now, however, the ducks had mostly departed, with other good things to eat, and the few that remained lived with the hens in the farmyard. The bridge, therefore, had gone the way of things that are no longer used. The rope was still there, still strong and fairly taut, but one hand wire had broken and could be seen in the water, curling away downstream, and the other, though still there, sagged in the middle until it was only half a yard from the rope.

They delivered their message, had a look at the twin calves that had been born that morning, and were moving off, when Krak caught sight of this relic of a bridge.

"Aha!" he cried, pleased as if he'd found a gold mine. "What's that? A bridge?"

"It *was* a bridge," said Bridget.

"It *is* a bridge. I cross it." And he did, bouncing over in some strange way of his own, sure-footed as a goat, and back again. "That is grand—" he beamed, "grand practice. It is P.T. It is trapeze. It is every sort of training. Try it."

"Not me," said Bridget; and Antosia suddenly sat down. But Krak wasn't taking "no" for an answer.

"But you must. Throw your arms out to balance and it is easy. You must—you altogether *must!*"

Now Bridget was good at gym and such things. She had a natural balance, a good head, and not too much imagination. She was so wet already that if she did fall into the river below, it wouldn't make her much wetter, and anyhow she liked water.

"All right. I altogether will," she cried, and started to waver across, hanging on tight to the hand wire, at times balancing beautifully, at times shuffling her feet sideways in frantic efforts not to be shaken off, at times over-balancing completely and sitting astride the rope, clinging, as it were, round its neck. James, barking like a lunatic dog, tore up and down the bank, imploring someone to save her.

Krak kept up a laughing, jeering stream of advice—"Up again—Bravo, Mademoiselle Blondin. See the famous tightrope dancer at practice—throw out the arm—you are O.K. —*up* again—"

"Get out, Krak, leave me alone. You're making it worse —hush up, James. Tossie, hang on to James, for goodness' sake. Oh, gosh! Have I got to go back again—I *can't*—" But she did. Rather pleased with herself, she went over,

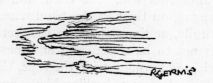

At times balancing beautifully

picked some loosestrife as a token, and came back to throw it and herself down beside Antosia, who was sitting silently watching, her hands clasping her knees.

"Good. Now, Antosia," cried Krak from the other side.

A shiver ran down Antosia from the crown of her head to the tips of her toes. Bridget saw it come as you see a wind rippling over still water. Her face was white, her hands were white, so tightly were they clasped. This bridge

was exactly the kind of thing she disliked most. She loathed
heights, crossing narrow planks, walking along the tops of
walls; and she abhorred water. The very idea of crossing
that bridge made her feel sick, as Bridget very well knew.

"Don't you dream of it, Tossie," she whispered, and
called back to Krak, "No. This sort of thing isn't Tossie's
street. She's not going near your beastly bridge."

"Oh, yes, she is," shouted Krak cheerfully, and he
added something in Polish that made Antosia leap to her
feet as if she'd been stung.

"Don't you do it, Tossie. Don't be an idiot!" cried
Bridget, but over she went, more skilfully perhaps than
Bridget herself, her dancer's muscles serving her well. She
did it in complete silence, though, her face as white as
milk, her teeth set. She gave the earth a stamp on the other
side, as if she hated it, and came back. Then she retired
behind a bush and was very sick.

"Another Mademoiselle Blondin!" cried Krak, and came
dancing across, balancing himself so that he hardly touched
the hand wire. "But where is she?"

A peculiar noise came from behind the bush.

"Eaten something," explained Bridget. Tossie would
never forgive her if she said anything else.

"Yes, eaten something." Antosia emerged with dignity,
her face still green. "And now drinking something." She
went to the edge of the stream, cupped her hand and drank.
"And now well again."

"Good," said Krak. "What shall we do now? Cross over
again?"

"No, I'm blessed if we do," said Bridget decidedly. "I've
had enough of that bridge. Let's go along that field path
and see where it takes us. It looks over to Skiddaw and

Tossie likes looking at mountains. Come on, Tossie, tell us a story while we go." Get away from that loathsome bridge into the realms of imagination, that was the thing to do. If only they had the blanket to crawl under as they had in the boat that torpedo time! She pulled Antosia's ice-cold, shaking hand through her arm, and, firmly hooked together, they started off.

Antosia warmed to the story at once.

"That," she said, "will not be Skiddaw, not an English mountain at all, it will be Czartorya. It is a huge, hollow cave of a mountain and in it a thousand knights in full armor are sleeping with all their horses and all their arms. A genie put them to sleep like your Sleeping Beauty when Silesia was torn from Poland. And every hundred years a knight comes to the mouth of the cave and looks out and cries, 'Is it time?' But it is not time, and he gives a sigh that blows over the forest and shivers the trees and he goes back—"

"Or does *not* go back!" cried Krak; and with that they slipped into Polish and were lost to Bridget. Let them, she said to herself; let them argue till they're blue in the face. Tossie was warming up again, her color was coming back, she had forgotten that awful bridge. In another minute she'd begin to sing about the Orava Road . . .

She did, and many another song, and they all went skipping along in the pouring rain until the water came through to their skins and their clothes had to spend the rest of the day hung up on Maggie's rail over the kitchen fire. So it was not such a bad walk, after all.

⇒ 3 ⇐

There was another day of rain, then came a roaring wind, drying up everything, and they went off, all three of them, to help with the job of the day, sheep dipping.

Krak and Ronnie had rounded them up, the poor sheep. There they were, huddled together in the pen put up around the dip, waiting until someone a lot stronger than themselves seized upon them and threw them into the loathsome water—or that was how Antosia saw it. In they went and someone poked their poor heads under, like a bathing woman ducking her bathers in the old illustrations. One splash and flounder and struggle, however, and they were out again, bundling up the ramp on their four feet on their way to dry land once more.

"Not so bad really," said Bridget, as she and Antosia stood there watching, James between them. (James had just had the first beating of his life for the awful offense of chasing sheep and he was still doubtful of them.) "It's soon over."

"Not at all soon for the sheep." Antosia's voice was warm with sympathy. "They stand there and Ronnie or Krak or someone pounces on them like a tiger and throws them in and they drown—that's what they think."

"But they don't drown—that's the whole point."

"They fear they will. It's the same."

"It isn't. If they were sensible, they'd just walk out again on the other side and it'd be done."

"But they're not sensible. They're sheep."

Krak's voice rang out.

"Now then, Antosia, let's see you try."

To Bridget's astonishment, Antosia at once hurled herself at the nearest sheep. It bundled away from her in the sudden, enormously violent way sheep have, and she was left clawing the air, only shreds of wool left in her hands.

"Ho, ho, ho!" jeered Krak, very much amused, and he roared out something in Polish that at once hurled Tossie at it again. This time she hung on for dear life, her teeth set, her mouth shut like a trap, and was dragged the length of the pen, most of the way on her knees in the mud, one boot off, her arms nearly pulled out of her sockets. This time everyone laughed good-naturedly.

"Defeat!" shouted Krak, and strode after the pair of them. He picked up the sheep in his arms like a great bundle of wool, carried it to the dip and dropped it in with a splash that sent showers on them all. "Victory!"

"He's strong, Antosia's uncle," said Mr. Firbeck, approvingly. "Never seen a stronger pair of arms."

"Yes," said Bridget, "but Tossie isn't. She couldn't lift that sheep any more than I could." There she was in the corner, quite pale, pulling her sleeves down, the blood trickling from her knee where it had caught the edge of a stone. Bridget went over to her. "What in the world did you go doing that for?"

"Krak said to try," mumbled Tossie angrily, and flung back her hair.

"Bunk. He didn't mean it. You might as well try to lift a cow. Here's your boot. There's a tap round the corner. What about getting the mud off while it's wet—"

But Krak called out something else and away Tossie flew.

Bridget shrugged her shoulders. It was the wire bridge all over again. If Tossie was going to have a shot at doing everything Krak did—well, she'd have to get up pretty early. Anyway, it was time for twelve o'clock dinner and Maggie had to be given a hand, so in Bridget went.

➤ 4 ◄

At dinner the question of the bore came up. It had rained for nearly twenty-four hours, there'd be a lot of water coming down the river, the wind was blowing half a gale, there'd likely be a grand bore, said Mr. Firbeck.

"A bore? What is that then?" inquired Krak at once.

"Mrs. Drake kept talking about the bore—what is it exactly?" Bridget was as keen to know as anyone.

Ronnie explained. When the river was a bit swollen and the tide was running high to meet it, with a good bit of wind behind it, then the sea came up with a rush, running along in a sort of wall. That was the bore, and the water would be over the banks and across the marsh in the flick of a cow's tail.

Antosia shivered and murmured, "It was a bore then that caught the Scots."

"Aye, it would be," agreed Ronnie. "Now what you'll want to do is to take the boat and ride it."

"Ride it? *Ride* the bore? But—" Krak's blue eyes glistened like a small boy's.

"I'd come myself but I've the cows to milk. Take her down lower, where the river narrows a bit."

"Where's the boat?"

"Drawn up. Blades saw to that."

"We'll get it down, the boat. We'll do this riding, shall we, Bridget?"

Wouldn't they! Just wouldn't they! If there was a thing

Bridget adored it was a boat.

"Yes, rather. My goodness, yes."

"And Antosia."

"No, not Tossie. She can watch and yell at us out of the window. She hates boats like poison—boats and tides and waves—"

And then, of all amazing things, if Antosia didn't flare up into one of her sudden furies and say she was coming, of course she was. Why couldn't she ride the bore as well as anyone else?

Bridget stared.

"But, Tossie, why on earth should you? You'll only—" Then she stopped, for Antosia had landed her a sharp kick under the table that meant "shut up." At the same moment Maggie came slanting in and ran round the table, collecting the pudding plates; dinner was done.

"You haven't finished your pudding, Grandmother Bridget. Hurry, hurry, hurry, and give us no more advice or you'll keep Maggie waiting." Antosia was pretending to laugh, but there was a steely glint in her eye. What in the world was she after? She couldn't *want* to come out in the boat—she'd loathe it. It would be a sort of torture—

Krak got up and lit a cigarette. "We shall want advice, Antosia, you and I, when it comes to boats. I fall out of boats, I catch crabs, I never—what do you call it?—trim a boat—"

Antosia was darting around, collecting tumblers. "Trim? You don't trim boats, you trim hats. You know no English, Krak, you should come to Ramparts—" And she flew off to the sink to wash up.

Bridget finished her pudding, completely mystified, did some drying and other odds and ends, then pursued Antosia into their bedroom.

"Now, look here, Tossie, I don't know what you're after but you're no earthly good in a boat and you can't swim and you hate the sight of water—what's the idea?"

Antosia was dragging on one of her long boots.

"There is no idea."

"It'll be cold and wet and you can't row . . . anyway Krak will be doing that, I'm sure. When the tide comes up it'll be nothing but water, like the sea—"

"No, no, *no!*" Antosia threw the other boot at Bridget's head, cast herself on the bed, face down, and kicked.

Bridget sat down gingerly on the edge of the bed.

"Tossie, what in the world's the good of—"

With another of her instant changes, Antosia whirled around, sat up, tossed her hair back, and burst into explanations.

"There *is* good. I must. It is necessary for me to do things. Krak tells me it is necessary. I must be able to do everything. My aunts—he saw my aunts in Warsaw—they travel across and across Poland in their work. They ride, they climb, they walk—"

"I bet they don't go riding bores."

"They ride anything," said Antosia with dignity. She swung her feet to the floor with her quick dancer's movements, and stood, the effect a little spoiled by having only one boot on. "Say no more, Grandmother."

Bridget frowned, unimpressed.

"I wouldn't say any more if you could swim. Daddy never let us into a boat hardly till we could swim. Does Krak know you can't swim?"

"He does not and if you dare to tell him—"

"Of course I shall tell him."

And at that came such a flood of commands, entreaties, tears, jibes, long sentences of wonderful common sense, jeers at being such a great grandmother—all Antosia's battery of persuasion going full blast—that at last Bridget gave way. All right, she wouldn't tell Krak that Antosia couldn't swim.

"Though I think you're an absolute simpleton."

"Why? What am I going to do? Nothing. Is it to be a simpleton to sit still in a boat while you and Krak row about and say 'How beautiful'? Very crazy, but not so crazy as the fuss you make about nothing. We do not spend eighteen days in it this time—it is what you call a boating party, a pleasure. Ugh!" Antosia made an indescribable grimace. "And afterwards I shall learn to swim."

"Oh, will you?" said Bridget skeptically. "Well, don't you go wearing those long boots."

"Why not? It's raining again. I like to keep dry," and Antosia pulled on the other.

But Bridget decided not to wear hers. Daddy had always been rather against rubbers in small boats. She pulled on two old sweaters and left her boots behind.

> 5 <

Krak had been quite right. He needed advice when it came to boats; it was soon apparent that he knew very little about them. But Ronnie was there with plenty, and he himself made up in muscle what he lacked in skill. They ran the little dinghy down to the water, got in, the three of them, and Ronnie pushed them off. They were in nice time, he said. "Keep her head on," he bawled, and made off to his cows.

But Krak was not too sure what "head on" meant. He had both oars and yet he rather fancied facing the way the bore was coming so that he could see it—how did you do that? "You didn't," said Bridget. Whereupon he gave a terrific pull and they shot into the current, spinning round like a top, the wind blowing the water up into waves, the boat ducking and bobbing and sidling, Krak roaring with laughter at it and himself. He might have been about eight, the way he shouted and half-sang, pulling on one oar and then the other, feathering one moment, digging like a gardener the next, the oars forever jumping out of the oarlocks.

My goodness, what would Daddy say, Bridget thought with horror as they zigzagged out. She had been brought up to have a respect for boats and their ways. If only she could have got hold of the oars . . . no good thinking of that, though. If Krak got up, attempted to move, it'd be an earthquake, and they'd upset for a certainty. Besides, he was enjoying himself; he wouldn't give them up for anything.

She took a look at Antosia. She wasn't enjoying it. No, she was not. She was sitting in the stern, arms outstretched, her knuckles white with holding on to the sides of the boat. Her legs in the long boots were stiff as pokers against the floor boards. With the state of tension she was in, her mouth was set in an extraordinary, meaningless grin. In another minute, thought Bridget, she'll be sick with fright—she always is—and then what shall we do?

And then the bore came.

It was not at all a large bore really; a low rushing wall of sea that spread behind into a waste of water, blotting out the marsh, the river banks, the river itself, turning the world into a brown ocean that seemed to stretch to the gray Scottish hills.

"Get her round! Head on!" shouted Bridget. But there was no "head on" about it. Krak had no more control over the boat than he had over the bore. He gave a mighty whoop of joy as they met it broadside, were lifted up, spun around, carried along, banged against a bit of hidden bank and carried along again. An oar leaped out of its oarlock, this time overboard. Krak lunged after it, his whole weight on one side, and—over they went . . .

The next thing Bridget knew was that Antosia had her by the plait, that thick rope of hair that she was never allowed to cut off. Tossie weighed a ton and it hurt like anything and they were both dipping under, choking and spluttering and fighting, so Bridget pushed her in the face until she let go, then screeched, "Kick, Tossie, kick them off," meaning the horrible boots she had insisted upon wearing—they were making her as heavy as lead. As soon as she understood, her wildcat kicks got them off. Bridget could hear Krak's mighty voice shouting further down. But Tossie kept slipping away.

"It's all right, I've got you," Bridget yelled whenever she could get the breath, and hung on to her friend for dear life. She had learned lifesaving, but, try as she would, she couldn't get hold of Antosia in the right way. It was easy enough in the baths, but awful here in this river. Out of the current—somehow she must get her out of the current and back to the swirl and eddy that meant the riverbank underneath. She grabbed and pulled and spluttered and swam and tried to hold up Tossie's white face—she never made a sound.

They thudded against something. Bridget felt her foot

strike land—and the next moment there they were, a couple of gasping fish stranded in a foot of water. The boat, the oars, Antosia's boots were bobbing away on the tide, Krak's head bobbing after them, all rapidly becoming specks in the distance.

≻ 6 ≺

That night Antosia came and sat on Bridget's bed. The wind was still whistling and roaring around Scaurbank's chimneys and instead of the river a brown lake stretched below the window.

"Tomorrow," she said, and she fetched up a deep sigh, "tomorrow you teach me to swim."

"I'm blessed if I do."

"Why not?"

"I'd as soon teach a half-drowned cat."

Antosia gave a long chuckle.

"It's all very fine to laugh but you were jolly nearly drowned."

"I should have been altogether drowned," said Antosia calmly, "if it had not been for your plait. It was my rope ladder, my life line, my anchor."

"Well, it's not going to be any of those things again, that's all I can say. It still hurts the way you pulled it. And why in the world wouldn't you let me tell the others what happened? When Krak said at supper what a grand day it had been and that he'd never enjoyed anything half so much in his life, why did you say 'yes, wasn't it!' when you knew you'd been sick for ages with nothing but fright?"

"Not *nothing* but fright. I swallowed a lot of water."

"Serves you right. And serves you right if there's another bore tomorrow and Krak wants to do it again."

Antosia sighed. "He does want to do it again tomorrow. More 'head on,' he says."

At that Bridget sat bolt upright.

"Now you listen to me. You're not going with him and that's flat. I won't have it. Mr. Firbeck's taking his pigs to market tomorrow and I'm going with him and you're coming, too. I'm not going to leave you with Krak, not for a moment."

"Grandmother Bridget—" But Tossie's voice was warm and grateful. "I will hold on tight to your plait and never let go." Then she made one of her sudden changes of mood. She seized Bridget by the shoulders and said in threatening tones, "Can you teach me to swim in five days?"

"No."

"But you must, you must, you must. Five days."

"Why? Why five?"

"Because Krak goes in seven days. On five days you teach me, very private, very secret, very security. Then on the sixth day we shall have a bathing party and I shall swim." She got up and floated gracefully about the room to show how beautifully she intended to swim.

"But . . . what *is* the idea?—I still don't know. Why must you do all these things you can't do—make yourself ill crossing that wire bridge, nearly break your arms trying to lift a sheep, getting yourself half-drowned riding the bore—why? Can't you tell me?"

Antosia went over to the window and put her head out. The wind was like the slip stream from an aeroplane, it blew her hair until it floated around her head like seaweed around a rock. She stayed there a moment, then came back and sat down again to answer the question.

"It is difficult—I can tell you very little because there is so little to tell. You would laugh and say, do you then travel by Metro or by the Tube, if I tell you I am to go 'underground.' Krak's mission was to the 'underground.' And to go underground you must have courage, courage, courage all the time. Krak is forever saying so. All kinds of courage—courage to make parachute jumps and also to be hungry, courage to swim in water you hate, to be strong and to win, to make yourself punctual, to remember exactly, not half-remember, courage to not be unhappy, to act—that is the only kind I have yet—" and she broke into a laugh that was half a sob, or a sob that was half a laugh —"but I must learn all the others."

Bridget stared. It was too dark to see Tossie's face, but this, she knew, was serious. This was "Poland" again. They were back at that evening after the Remove show.

"But you've tons of courage, Tossie. Simply tons. Look at Mrs. Drake's bull."

"Bull nothing—I was not afraid. It is courage when you *are* afraid I must have, Krak says."

"But you can't possibly help it if you're afraid of some things—"

"You can. Krak says you can. He was afraid. He was sick all night before his first jump, but he is not sick any more now. Training, he says, and your courage grows."

"But it's all very fine for Krak to talk—you're a girl—"

"That makes no difference, he says, no difference at all. It is different for you, Bridget. You are English, you can be what you are. There is no hurry for you to change yourself. But for me, I must. I am not at all brave—"

"Yes, you are. Look at that bull—"

"*Stop* about the bull—I am used to bulls, I have lived on a farm—" and the argument went on.

Bridget never forgot that night and the conversation that wound itself round and round into a ball and stopped only to start all over again from the beginning; nor the dry-land swimming lesson that finally finished it, with Antosia balanced on a chair striking out with arms and legs—"*One-two, one-two*—have I got it, Bridget? Oh, if it was not *water*, how easy—" At last she was dragged to bed. "Tomorrow—early—we go swimming, *one-two*, one-two . . ." she murmured from the depths of her pillow.

"No, we don't," grunted Bridget from hers.

"Tomorrow and every morning I wake you. I learn to wake myself . . . I learn to set a clock in my head, Krak says . . ." and at last silence fell.

In one minute, it seemed to Bridget, Maggie was screaming below their window that it had gone eight, the little pigs had been washed and Ronnie was putting them into the trailer—didn't they hear the noise? Were they going to market or not? And did they want any breakfast or not?

Antosia did it. She learned to swim—after a fashion—in her five days. The bathing party with Krak came off and was a success, though there were some bad moments.

"Now I challenge you to a race across the river. I give you a start of—how much? Bridget, say how much start I give Antosia—you are very what you call 'fair'—"

But Bridget's attack of "cramp"—she had seen her father get cramp and she knew exactly how to act it—got Antosia out of the water in time.

"You're not the only one who can act," Bridget whispered, screwing up her face into the correct spasms. "Rub it—stretch out my leg and rub it, go *on*—" and Krak had to swim across alone.

"And what did you do with Uncle Krak all day?" inquired Grannie, when, a day or two later, they were back at Green Hedges and Scaurbank was rapidly misting over into a dream of glorious holidays.

"Well," said Bridget truthfully, "it wasn't so much what we did with him as what he did with us. It was very interesting."

"Great fun, I'm sure."

"Yes, great fun," said Antosia.

ANTOSIA TAKES
A JOURNEY

R.GERVIS

Chapter VIII

➤ 1 ◄

THEY sat in the Long Hall, waiting for Addy. The September light streamed in on the Romney *Reading Lady*, glowing softly on her cream-colored skirts, lighting her absorbed face under her big cap as she bent over her book. You looked at her, Antosia said, and "everything came together." What exactly she meant by that remark Bridget could never make out. You didn't explain, Tossie said, when you looked at pictures. The Lady was still and she was reading; my goodness, she was reading! She paid no attention to Addy who would soon be standing in front of her; or to Ramparts who sat in a body, solidly staring at her because for the moment they found nothing else to look at. She had her own life, Tossie said; she was beautiful and the shadowy folds of the satin were lovely past compare . . . it would be easier, if one had to talk about her at all, to say it in French. But that, Bridget reflected, was exactly like Tossie. All sorts of ideas ran round in her head, ideas she never quite pinned down into words. All the

same, she was right, the more one looked at pictures the
more one *did* look at them; at first one didn't see them at
all—though Tossie had from the beginning. Even on that
awful first day in the air-borne suit she had hardly taken
her eyes off the Van Dyck boy. And at the memory of
that day Bridget still shuddered. It had been a near thing;
she could hear the echoes of Addy's "Nevertheless . . ."
even now. And here they were, both in the Upper Fifth—
gosh, she could hardly believe it! Both of them practically
fifteen. Two years since the torpedo put them in the same
boat; two years since the ship's cook made Tossie's birthday cake with the Polish flag and the thirteen dates sticking up like tombstones . . . ages and ages . . .

Addy walked springily in, brown as any of them; she had
been harvesting too. She made her opening speech as she
always did at the beginning of every term. It was now
1943, she said, and the war very far from over . . . ar-
rangements had been made to continue war work by every
possible means. Would members of the Sixth and Upper
Fifth put their names down for the hospital orderly rota,
for helping with the Shernham Guides and Brownies, for
canteen, or farm work. Upper Fifth—that's us, thought
Bridget, with a feeling of amazement that it should be so.
What had they better do? Farm work, perhaps. Or Tossie
might like the Brownies—she adored small kids, and she'd
make them dance and act.

"We must congratulate Christabel Wood on her Somer-
ville History scholarship—" *work* . . . the Certificate
would be looming . . . gosh, how frightful. What would
Tossie do about that? Have a shot, probably—Krak would
certainly say have a shot. But Krak was a long way from
Ramparts, about as far as Scaurbank.

Now Addy was reading out subjects for the Debating Society—they'd be in that now, and wouldn't Tossie talk! Just *wouldn't* she! Equal Pay for men and women, Basic English, Is Ambition a Virtue? she wouldn't mind what it was. Now they'd reached the games, then a bit of uplift and Addy would be done. The hockey team. They were both in—and, mercy, if she, Bridget, wasn't vice-captain! If it hadn't been that the whole form led by Tossie exploded into grins and pats on the back, she wouldn't have believed it. A nice lot of matches—some new ones, the Waafs from the neighboring Unit, a factory team from Shernham, the Y.W., who would probably be fearfully good . . . "And now here we are, at the beginning of our school year with all its hopes and aspirations and opportunities before us . . ."

Addy was good at this sort of thing; Ramparts knew it. They were always very pleased and proud when they read in the paper, "The prizes were distributed by Miss Adams, the Headmistress of Ramparts, whose stirring speech . . ." "Miss Adams, the Head of the well-known girls' school, in an inspiring address . . ." "Miss Adams of Ramparts, well known as a speaker in the educational world, kept her delighted audience in fits of laughter . . ." and so on.

"Here's another lot Sent Up," they said when they picked up the paper, but if it dared to say, as happened sometimes, "Miss Adams gave the address," and nothing more, they were furious. Now they listened as connoisseurs, but, nevertheless, wholeheartedly while she expounded what exactly she expected of them in the immediate future. Bridget, like everyone else, was "enthused"; it was going to be a grand term, the best yet. As for Antosia, she pranced out, treading on air—*See my chestnut bounding,* she was almost singing it aloud . . .

Ten minutes to talk, to find out what the others had been up to, Judy and Toinette, Elspeth MacDonald and Rosemary Parke and the rest of them. Then off to their new room, new form mistress, new work, new term.

> 2 <

Grannie took a great interest in all this. It was as if, she said, she were back at Ramparts herself. Bridget had caught up her ancestors; gone beyond them in fact if she intended to take the Certificate before she was sixteen.

"Are you really taking it? And is Antosia?"

"They decide for certain at Christmas, it depends on exams. Then either we go in for it in July or we wait till Christmas in a special sort of Certificate form."

"Like geese being fattened," said Antosia. "Addy says I'll perhaps wait forever."

"Rubbish," said Grannie cheerfully.

"That's because of her history."

"She takes European history, I suppose. Don't you know any, Antosia?"

"She knows far too much, Addy says. What she's got to work at is forgetting."

"Hm." Grannie was interested in this. "It is certainly something a country must learn—what in their history to remember and what to forget. No good driving back to the horses all the time, looking behind."

Antosia frowned. "I should like to do English history then I needn't try to forget—Henry the Eighth and his wives, Charles and Nell Gwyn. But Addy says no."

"Sensible woman. All the ridiculous scraps of misinformation you've picked out of the films would ruin you. What else are you doing this term?"

Any amount. Bridget, as vice-captain, was on the Games Committee and a very select Selection Committee of three, herself, the Captain and the Games Mistress. She was already full of lists and time sheets and ground plans. In the future, she determined, no vestige of talent should escape her eye. That kid in the Lower Fourth has three brothers; she runs like a boy . . . she was already saying to herself; Susan, a Sixth, has gone a bit heavy, she's not going to be any good right wing—what about trying her in goal? Bridget had a good many hours of conscientious watching and playing in other people's games before her.

Antosia was busy in a different way. Her dramatic club was again in being and now included the Lower Fifth. It had blossomed out into a special dancing section; she was teaching them the Robber Dance and Elspeth was teaching them Scottish reels. She was learning the Sword Dance herself. "But I shall never do it. Feet, feet, feet, nothing but feet. No arms, no head, no smiles, all so still except for the crowing, like cocks at dawn—"

"And next summer, Grannie, the school is going to do *As You Like It*, the first real play since the war began," Bridget broke in. "I think Addy's rather bucked about Tossie's club because it'll help her to find out who can act and who can't. Then we're picking up potatoes five days from two to four for a fortnight, and Tossie's going to some Brownies on Saturday mornings, and our form's adopted a mine sweeper and we're all going to knit like mad. Eleven pairs of gloves—*gloves*, frightfully difficult—"

"A pretty busy term in front of you, in fact," said Grannie.

"Busy and beautiful," said Antosia. "And also there's Judy's scholarship."

Judy was a relic of Antosia's Remove, and partly because of that and partly because she had helped with that first dramatic effort, Tossie took her and her scholarship very seriously indeed. Judy took it seriously too, goodness knows she did. She had worked like fury in the holidays and her pieces were more or less ready. All she wanted, Antosia told her, was the "Plus," like the dog in the advertisement. "You have to become a plus dog. You must play to win, you must never stop and say, 'Sorry,' when you forget. You must never let the *zip* go, you must feel and feel and not think when you play. Come now and play to me. How many examiners do you have?"

"Four, I think."

"Then I will be all four. I will be first a very old and bald one and you will play me your Bach, the *English Suite*, while I sit in a chair. Then I will be a not so old one with gray hair all ruffled up and eyebrows like fur and you will play me the *Beethoven Sonata* while I walk about. Then I will be a much younger one with tortoise shell spectacles and a big white forehead and long hands, and you will play me the *Polonaise* while I look out of the window. And last of all I will be young and square with my hair *en brosse* and you will play the modern piece while I stare at you."

"Antosia! How do you know all that?"

"I asked that new music mistress. She tried for one. Now come and begin. D'you see them, the four?"

It was one thing to see Antosia as these four terrifying gentlemen and laugh at her portraits of them, but it was quite another to satisfy her on their behalf.

"Mr. A. did not like your Bach. It is like a tap running, he says, and he fell asleep. You must *brisk* it. Mr. C. says the *Polonaise* should make him want to pick up a sword and rush into the street, but instead he puts on his slippers— If he's looking out of the window and wears spectacles—"

Judy might protest, but there was no good arguing with Antosia. She talked twice as fast and twice as much as anyone else, and she acted the four examiners, voice, manner, acid comments and all until you felt they were there.

"And when is it that you meet these alarming gentlemen?" asked Grannie, when Antosia had brought Judy to Green Hedges for a change of audience—"who, I may say, you will probably find most amiable and genial and charming and unlike Antosia."

"First week in December." And Judy shivered.

"Don't do that, Judy. You mustn't shiver or shudder. You must say I can, I will, I shall, I *do*."

"I wish you'd come with me, Antosia."

"I will, if Addy lets me off."

"Addy doesn't let people off, you know quite well she doesn't. She never gives us a night, even at half term."

"No. She's a strict old thing. Now play again and Grannie can be the examiners and I'll listen and enjoy every note. It's lovely, Judy. When you play the Bach I feel like the *Reading Lady* over the platform, quiet and happy and in a satin dress like parchment." And with that Tossie became the perfect listener and Judy felt full of confidence and ease, as if she had *Nelly Bly* to play to a kindergarten.

And Antosia was very nearly as keen on Rosemary Parke, who was now allowed hockey and had to be coached up and at all costs squeezed into the form eleven. And on Toinette, who had the sweetest singing voice and who would probably be given the part of Amiens in *As You Like It* when the time came and sing *Blow, blow, thou winter wind,* if only they could get her accent better.

"Stop her, you must stop her, Bridget, when she goes too French. Make her say your r's. Go on, Toinette, *Round the rugged rocks the ragged rascals ran*—now listen, and say it like Bridget. Go *on*—" and then came a flood of French to tell her how she must go on and on and *on*, and they'd never leave her alone till she did.

Oh, how keen Tossie was on everything and everybody! The term was flying along—hurtling along, you might say, with all the crowd of things they were doing, hockey matches, debates, washing up in the hospital kitchen, Judy's piano, Toinette's English, the dramatic club, the dancing that the whole school were going mad about.

The wheel of Ramparts is fairly whizzing round, said Bridget to herself, remembering her first impressions, she and Tossie with it—and in what a place, in what a perfectly glorious place! Not on the outside edge any more but right in the middle, close to the hub . . .

And that was what made it all the more astounding that Antosia should suddenly disappear.

> 3 <

Bridget and James were awakened by what sounded like the click of a latch. James, no longer such a young dog now, cocked his ear and gave a short, questioning yelp. Bridget sat up. It was nearly December and mornings were dark. Half past six. No need to move yet. Breakfast was

James cocked his ear and gave a short yelp

laid overnight these days. Grannie never bothered to come down until she felt like it. Washing up didn't matter, with Mrs. Drake "changed" as she was by the bull—the Blessed Bull as Grannie called it.

Bridget lay down again—she must have imagined that click—snoozing and vaguely considering the events of the coming day. Rather a good day it was going to be; Addy's literature lesson, which always had a kick about it; a pick-up match with players carefully chosen by the Games Mistress, herself one of the captains; Tossie's dancing club after tea doing an eightsome. Yes, rather a particularly good day, as it happened.

Bridget slipped on her dressing gown and went down to put the kettle on. No signs of Antosia—naturally. She could get up punctually when she liked—witness the tennis practice and those frightful swimming lessons—but there was no reason for it today. Very often she appeared dressed, ready to start, and ate her breakfast while Bridget fetched the bicycle from the shed.

When, however, ten minutes to eight came and still Antosia wasn't there, Bridget went up to her room to say sternly, as she always did, "Tossie, you're going to be late and I won't wait for you."

She opened the door and began, "Tossie—"

But there was no Tossie. The bed was made, the room was unnaturally tidy. It didn't look as if Antosia had slept there for weeks!

That click as of the front door came back to Bridget. She and James had heard it then. What in the world was Tossie after, starting for school at that unearthly hour? Or if not for school—

Struck with a sudden misgiving, Bridget went to the cupboard and opened it. The Ramparts uniform was hanging there, for once properly on its hanger; but the blue Sunday suit had gone, and Tossie's best shoes. And the airborne beret. And the little traveling bag that Krak had given her.

Bridget went down again, shouted good-bye under Grannie's window, as they always did, and rode off to Ramparts in a dream.

Antosia wasn't in hall—Bridget hadn't expected that she would be.

"Isn't she coming?" "Is she *bad?*" "Nothing infectious, is it?" The form instantly made up their minds Tossie was ill. "A pity—you'll have to do with Violet on your left wing and she's slow, you know—" said the Games Mistress.

Addy, going out after the literature class, said, "Tell Antosia I missed her. I meant her to read the Shelley to us—and, by the way, tell that delightful grandmother of yours that she's supposed to write me a letter as parent or guardian when a pupil is absent. I don't suppose she knew, as you've never missed a day, either of you. I hope it's nothing much."

So Tossie was ill. Well, any moment she might walk in and then she could explain for herself. She *might*. Or she might not. She might never walk into Ramparts again!

Bridget had the first hour off, when she was supposed to go to the library and read. Instead, she nipped on her bicycle and flew off to Shernham station, where she had a friend among the porters, Drake's nephew.

"Good morning, Bob," she said, as if she hadn't a care in the world. "You didn't notice my Polish friend, I s'pose, this morning?"

"Yes, miss, I did. Caught the 7:35 all right. We didn't half run for it. It was movin' but I got a door open and had her by the arm and in she went like a rabbit."

"Oh. I wondered."

"Near thing. Never seen nearer. And couldn't do nothing but laugh, she couldn't."

After that Bridget had a bad, glum morning and lost herself through Break to avoid questions, hiding most of the time in the boot room, peaceful this time of day, where she could sit looking at the rows of shoes, asking them, "Where has she gone? Where *has* she gone? Why didn't she tell me?" till it was time to go to her form and sit like a daytime owl through a French lesson.

At quarter to one, the morning over, her spirits down to zero, Bridget took her way up to the loathsome little room at the top of the stairs.

"Come in," said Addy in a grim, professionally displeased voice. "*You*, Bridget?" Her eyebrows shot up.

"I'm—I'm not sent up," said Bridget hastily.

"I should hope not indeed. What is it?"

"It's about Tossie—"

"Antosia."

"Antosia, I mean. I wanted to tell you—Grannie didn't send a note because she doesn't know she hasn't come."

"Hasn't come?"

"Isn't here—isn't at school."

"*What?*"

It was an unpleasant quarter of hour. Why hadn't Bridget told her grandmother? Why hadn't she told her form mistress? Why had she waited till *now* . . . ? "D'you mean to tell me that Antosia has just gone off without giving you the slightest hint she was going?"

"Not the slightest."

"But where has she gone?"

"I don't know."

"And why?"

"I don't know."

"But, Bridget, you give me the impression that you *do* know."

"I don't."

"You're guessing then."

"Well, of course—no one can help guessing. Anyone would try to guess."

"I'm trying and I can't, whereas you can. You've something to go upon. What is it? Sit down and tell me." There was no second chair; at the awful interviews in that room the sinner stood. "Sit on the desk then and listen to me. Where is that uncle at this moment?"

Addy was like a thrush after a particularly long worm, digging at it with her clever, prodding questions, surmises, suggestions. At last she dragged out all Bridget knew of "underground" and her sickening fear that Antosia might be gone to become part of it, that she might have been whisked away by Krak or some such person to this mysterious other life, whatever it was, and be lost to them forever.

"What? Without saying a word to you?"

"If it was security, yes."

Addy bit on a pencil as if she were in the Lower Fourth and hummed like a bee for a moment or two. Then she shook her head and out it came.

"No. It's not that. She's too young. And it would be overdoing the secrecy altogether—no uncle in his senses would arrange such a thing. Besides, she has only taken a small bag, you say. No. It's nothing so grand as that. It's some impulse of her own. Now what? *What*, Bridget?"

The displeased note was back again, stronger than ever. She was annoyed with Tossie; not worried but annoyed. Bridget, reassured but anxious now in a different way, thrashed about for the right thing to say.

"It's not just anything, I'm sure. It's something that matters. She'll let us know—telephone or something. Antosia would never leave these things—the dancing this evening and the match—unless it was something frightfully urgent—"

"Hm. I wonder." Addy got up; the interview was at an end. "Well, the finding of her is your grandmother's responsibility, not mine. The question as to what she will do when found is, however, mine; whether she will remain at Ramparts—"

"Oh, but—"

"Or not."

There was something very final about the way Addy said that "not." Nothing more was to be said on Tossie's behalf for the moment.

Bridget slid off the desk.

"Had she—had she better still be ill? They think she's ill."

Addy became human again for an instant.

"No. No fibbing is necessary. If they believe she has a cold—only a cold, I think—let them. No doubt she forgot her coat—"

"She did."

"Well, then by now she probably has one."

She sat down and took up her pen. Bridget was dismissed.

> 4 <

Grannie was worse. When very sweet-tempered people are angry they are all the more alarming because one has had no practice in dealing with them. Grannie was angry with them both, Antosia for going off, Bridget for saying nothing about it until now. "It simply means I can't trust you, either of you, though you are in the Upper Fifth and vice-captain and all the rest of it. I'm *most* disappointed in you both. And now the fire's gone out."

The fire was the last straw. Grannie in her W.V.S. uniform had had an exhausting day, finding new billets for some of her less contented Londoners. She had looked forward to a comfortable tea with the latest Ramparts news to amuse her—and now this.

"It's so ungrateful of Antosia to do such a thing—I'm amazed at her. Even if she can take care of herself, as you say she can, it's very worrying, very worrying indeed. Where has she gone? What is she doing? Why doesn't she let us know? If you're so sure the fire isn't out, why don't you hold the paper up in front of it?"

It was a comfort to have the fire to coax. Tea was made,

Tossie's place was there, naturally, as no one knew she
had gone. Would she perhaps walk in and apologize beautifully and make Grannie laugh and they'd all be happy
again? Oh, if only she would! Bridget got *The Times* and
held it across the black fireplace, James watching with great
attention. How lucky dogs were to understand so little; he
just wanted the fire to burn, nothing more. Grannie knew
nothing about the "Underground" and Tossie, and Bridget
felt as if nothing would make her explain it all over again.
Besides, she was too angry to listen. She leaned back in
her armchair and flapped her gloves against the arm. . . .
Gone to London, probably—was there a particular film or
play she wanted to see?—or the ballet perhaps? More than
likely—Antosia went so mad about things. Very, very
naughty. Or was it that Uncle? Or a friend of that Uncle?
"Now don't you tell me, Bridget, it's a young man, someone else in a plum-colored cap with blue wings on his
sleeve—"

Bridget's eye, wandering unhappily about the paper in
front of her, lit on a modest heading— "Polish Parachutists'
Flag from Warsaw." She read the paragraph below to the
accompaniment of Grannie's weary, vexed voice.

*Polish Parachutist Units stationed in Scotland are to be
presented tomorrow with their regimental colors which
have been embroidered secretly by Polish women in Warsaw. A courier of the underground movement arrived re-
cently in Great Britain with the colors which he had
smuggled out of Poland. The flag, bearing the white cross
on a red background, is embroidered in gold, and bears the
motto of the parachute unit: "To Poland by the Shortest
Route."*

The fire behind the paper suddenly exploded into life

with a tall fierce flame that licked up the solid *Times* from top to bottom.

"Take care, child!" screamed Grannie.

"It's all right, it's all right!" cried Bridget, and fought for her precious paragraph, tearing it out with the flames darting at her fingers and hot papery ashes floating around her like black moths.

"Look at you—can't even get the fire to burn without ruining my *Times*—I hadn't nearly finished it. You might be seven. Really, Bridget—"

"Look, Grannie, this is where Tossie's gone."

"What d'you mean? Don't let those ashes blow about the room—"

"Read it, Grannie darling—I'm sure it's Tossie—"

Grannie took the blackened strip and read. The fire crackled joyfully, red and yellow plumes racing up the chimney. Rouge lay down happily on the hearth rug; James sat bolt upright, as close as possible, and blinked at it. Happiness came surging back—it was as if Tossie herself had come to life with that flame and was back in her place. Krak's unit was stationed in Scotland. She'd gone to see that presentation. Clear as daylight. Bridget poured herself out a cup of tea and took a scone. Suddenly she was ravenous.

"But do you really think so?" asked Grannie.

"I'm certain."

"Why?"

"I just am."

The telephone rang; a telegram coming over. *A million apologies I return directly Antosia.* Handed in at Edinburgh.

"She'd no business to do it," said Grannie. "Put a log on the fire."

> 5 <

The newspaper cutting was carefully trimmed and cleaned up with a rubber and handed to Miss Adams by Bridget the next morning. She also had had a telegram from Edinburgh—*a thousand million regrets and apologies for absence returning shortly Antosia.* Antosia's penitence ran into astronomical figures, Miss Adams remarked, and handed it over in exchange.

"You're sure she read this?"

"Pretty sure. Antosia reads the paper like anything."

"Why—if you're right and this is where she's gone—why didn't she ask my permission?"

"She knew she wouldn't get it," said Bridget. Hadn't she heard Judy say so over the question of the scholarship and Tossie agreeing and saying Addy was a strict old thing. "You wouldn't have given it, would you?"

"No," said Addy after consideration. "Probably I shouldn't. But why not tell you?"

"I expect she thought I'd lock her in."

"And would you have locked her in?"

"Well . . ." How try to tell Addy what that ceremony would mean to Antosia? "No, I don't think I would."

Miss Adams was interested in this.

"Well, you're honest anyway."

"I would have if she'd been English and it was the Union Jack they were presenting. We don't need to go running after that sort of thing. We've got it. We've got it safe. We don't have to smuggle our flags. But it's quite different for Antosia. She hasn't got her country safe. It's like a drink when you're thirsty or bread when you're hungry for her to see Poles and a Polish flag and hear the Polish music and all that—she'd feel she must go to that show, whatever happened. I know she would. And I wouldn't have stopped her. No, I wouldn't."

Bridget was breathless. With Addy's cool, considering eyes on her, she wasn't saying it at all well.

"Hm. You're a very good Prisoner's Friend, I'll say that for you." Then out came the dreaded word— "Nevertheless . . ." Miss Adams shook her head and walked away, the cutting in her hand.

The form were easy. Bridget just said, "Tossie'll be back tomorrow or the next day," and let them think the cold was lifting. The dancing had been postponed—there was no good going on with it without Antosia. Would she be back if they had it after tea tomorrow, the form wanted to know. She might, Bridget thought; and she hurried off the moment work was over, as though she had hours of carrying trays and making beef broth before her.

Antosia's home-coming wasn't going to be too pleasant. Bridget did what she could by paving the way with Mrs. Drake—Drakey, as she had now become.

"Drakey, I'm afraid they're all rather ratty with Antosia."

"What's that for?" Mrs. Drake nowadays was always inclined to bristle if anyone criticized Tossie.

"Well, she took French leave and went off for a day or so."

"Oh, the bad girl."

"Not bad, but not too good. She's coming back from Edinburgh—I daresay by the night train. If she turns up while I'm at school, will you get hold of her—before Grannie sees her, mind—and make her change quickly and come along."

"Your Grannie's out to lunch every day this week."

"So she is—canteen. Someone's away. That's a bit of luck. You'll get hold of her the moment she comes, won't you? You'll see her get out of the bus, even if you've gone home."

"When'll it be?"

"I don't know. Change at Crewe, I suppose, like we did coming from Scaurbank, and get on as soon as there's a train. Tell her to go to the boot-room and wait there for me. Tell her to simply *slink* in and not speak to a soul till she's seen me. You'll get hold of her, won't you, Drakey? It'll make all the difference in the world if you do."

After all, there was no good in Tossie's coming back thinking it was all going to be plain sailing either with Addy or Grannie. You can't go nipping off from school, even to see flags presented, without paying the bill, and the quicker Antosia recognized that fact the better.

Bridget had a better morning after that arrangement was made. She spent break waiting in the boot-room and looked in there again at twelve o'clock, on her way to the library.

As dinner finished, the Captain strolled up. "There's a kid in the Lower Fifth I want you to see, Bridget. She's pretty fast—a lot faster than Violet anyway—shall we try her left wing if Antosia isn't better?"

"She is better— Half a minute—" cried Bridget, and flew off again.

This time Antosia was there, hunched up on the top of the row of pigeonholes, eating a cake in a ruminative sort of way, her hair falling across her face as it used to before

Ramparts made her get a slide. She jumped up when she saw Bridget, giving a little scream of welcome and relief.

"Drakey said the boot-room—but why *boots* when it is shoes we wear? I have never sat here in all my life. I thought she must be wrong when I waited and waited and you never came. She wouldn't let me stay a minute at Green Hedges. Hardly did she let me wash my face. She gave me a scone and a cake but I have had no breakfast and no dinner—"

"Tossie, did you go to see that Polish flag presented?"

Antosia stared. "Yes. How did you know?"

"I read about it in the paper."

"Oh, clever, clever, clever! I said to myself, Bridget will know, she'll think, she'll guess, she'll understand. Oh, Bridget, it was—" She stood there, her hands clasped, words failing her. Then she blew a kiss to the audience of shoes, danced a few steps, marched a few more, and sang something in Polish. "It was like that."

Bridget sat down, refusing to be impressed or sympathetic.

"It's all very fine but they're all frightfully sick with you."

"Ratty. Drakey said ratty. What's ratty? Two long teeth, long tail . . . see how they r-r-run . . ." She was airy enough, but her eyes had an anxious look in them, and her face was very white.

"Angry. Annoyed with you. Addy is, too. She's been nevertheless like anything."

"But you told her? You explained to her that I had to go?"

"Yes, I did. In a way. I don't think I did much good,

though. And all Grannie said was, 'She oughtn't to have done it!' "

"But I ought, I ought! Oh, Bridget, my two aunts helped to make that flag. Their initials were in the corner with the others. It went round from house to house, creeping in the dark—Krak had arranged all that when he went to Poland. And my father helped to get it out of the country. Oh, Bridget, just to look at that flag and take it in your hands—I should have been working at it. My cousin, who is younger than I, put in her stitches and there was her M., very small, for Marya. Krak was angry, too, when he heard I had come without the permission but he knew I *had* to see it. You know, too. They presented it and knelt to take it as if it was indeed very special, and the band played and I cried and cried till I could hardly sing—"

Antosia's eyes, what with hunger, remembered emotion and tiredness, were filling with tears.

"Now look here, Tossie, you've got to go up and see Addy the moment you come—that's what she said. She may easily fire you out of Ramparts—"

"Oh, no, *no*—"

"She may. Easily. It's a Council Rule, no leave of absence, specially put in for wartime. Here's my hanky—you stay here a moment and I'll go and get you something to eat. We've only just finished dinner, there was heaps of apple pudding left and that's one you specially like. You'll stand up to Addy a lot better if you're not hungry."

"Yes, Grandmother," said Tossie meekly, and mopped her eyes.

While the pudding was going down it was easier to explain Addy's point of view. She couldn't, after what the

Council ruled, have people dashing off to see flags without permission—

"But she wouldn't give it—I knew she wouldn't give it."

"Yes, I told her that. I'm not sure that it doesn't make it worse."

"But what else could I do?"

"Do without."

"*Oh!*" Antosia's outraged scream rang around the boot-room.

"That's what she'll say. You'd better come along and get it over. You're all right now. Here's my slide for your hair and a comb."

"But what do I say?" Antosia was rapidly tidying up.

"Apologize. Tell her the truth. Describe it—yes, describe it a lot. What the flag was like, what you felt like, what Krak had done, and your father and your aunts and the cousin and the whole lot of them. Put it on thick about the initials and all—" They were now on the way up to the horrid little room at the top of the stair.

"Don't forget you're supposed to have a cold—that's why you've been away. If we meet anyone, mind you put it on."

"Oh, I'll do that."

They ran into the Head Girl halfway up the stairs and Antosia's volley of sneezes echoed over the whole building.

"My goodness, you *have* got the father and mother of a cold, haven't you."

"Keeb away frob be," Antosia coughed wearily. "Dod't catch it."

"Better tomorrow," said Bridget and dragged her away.

"Do I have a cold for Addy?" she whispered.

"No, no. Take it off quick!"

"Not Paradise?"

"No."

"Am I sent up?"

"Rather. Capital S, capital U."

Antosia gave a short wail in Polish. "You'll come in with me?"

"No, 'fraid not."

"Oh, then give me your plait to hold, my anchor, my life line—" She clutched at Bridget's hair.

"No, we're not in the same boat this time, thank goodness."

"Oh, my blanket—my lucky sixpence—"

"Tossie, it's *serious*. Stop shivering and giggling. Pull yourself together and think what you're going to say. Go on, stand up straight and *think*. I'm going to knock."

"Come in," said Addy in her "sent up" voice.

"Antosia," announced Bridget, and closed the door.

NEW VOYAGES

Chapter IX

>- 1 -<

WHAT exactly happened inside that closed door, Bridget was never told. She waited in the boot-room, as they had arranged, and she seemed to wait a very long time. When at last Antosia appeared her face was bright pink, her eyes were glistening, and she carried her head with a challenging tilt to it, proud as a peacock.

Golly, there's been a battle, thought Bridget. And she asked anxiously, "Well, are you staying all right?"

"Yes, I am."

"Hooray!"

"But Addy's promised to read a history of Poland."

" 'But'? Why do you say 'but'?"

"Because it is 'but.' "

Tossie's voice was surprisingly warlike.

"I say, you did apologize to her for going off like that without permission, didn't you?"

"Yes, of course I did. But after that was done I told her why I had to go—you said I was to, so I did. And I told her a lot about Poland she didn't know. She didn't know about our lovely Queen of fifteen, our Jadwiga—she didn't *know!*" Antosia seemed amazed and scandalized at such ignorance. "I told her about Ladislas, too, who was killed fighting the Turks, and about all the people we're proud of —we are proud of them, just as you are of your good Queen Bess and your wonderful old Victoria. And I told her we were a great nation with a country that stretched all the way from the Baltic to the Black Sea when Russia and Prussia were little nothings of states and England was just a beautiful little wet island full of barbarians—"

"But not surely—" Bridget wasn't ready to swallow as much as that.

Antosia rushed on. "When all your Plantagenets were going on, you weren't anything like so civilized as we were—" Antosia began to get heated again— "You were hardly civilized at all compared to us, we began *centuries* before you. I'll tell you. In the beginning there were three Polish brothers, Lech and Czech and Rus. Czech went west and Rus went east and Lech went north till he found the nest of a white eagle, and he took the eagle as his emblem and we still have it, it's our Polish Eagle—we had it long before you had your lion—"

"But Richard Coeur de Lion—"

"That was only the Crusades, only the other day—"

Only the other day! Bridget gave up arguing and tried to be soothing. "I bet Addy knows all about that. History's her line, you know."

"If she did, then she has forgotten. She says some history must be forgotten, but I say never, never, *never*. She says new countries rise up and sweep over the world like a tide —always you English must talk about tides, about your cold and wet and horrible sea that takes people like us and drowns us—" Her voice was shaking and her face was scarlet.

"It doesn't if you're in a boat and if you've learned to swim—and you have learned to swim."

A faint snort rewarded Bridget's efforts to turn the conversation to something lighter; those swimming lessons at Scaurbank were usually guaranteed to raise some sort of a laugh, however Tossie felt. But not today. On she went again, faster, hotter, louder than ever. She couldn't stop talking, she was so tired. Poor Tossie, what between the fatigue and excitement of the flag business and the battling with trains in the blackout, no sleep and no breakfast, and then more battling with Addy on top of it all, she was half-dead, as Bridget clearly saw.

She picked up her coat which she had thrown down when they went upstairs and shoved Tossie into it.

"Now shut up about Poland and Rus and Lech and all the rest of them and come along back to Green Hedges and have tea. Drakey's made a cake specially for you. And drop scones. And I shouldn't be surprised if she didn't open a jar of that black currant jelly. And Grannie won't be back till supper so we'll have it to ourselves—and anyway she'll be so pleased to see you that she'll forgive you anything. We did miss you so—it was horribly dull without you. Now stop thinking about Addy and what she said and what you said and what you might have said and all that and just remember that you're staying on at Ramparts and that's what matters."

"That's what matters? It's having Grandmother Bridget's plait to hang on to that matters. Oh, Bridget!" Her voice was still doing funny things, breaking and half-sobbing, but she was comforted, Bridget could see.

They walked home arm in arm because Tossie hadn't a bicycle, Bridget chattering away as hard as she could about all their affairs. The hockey match with the new forward who wasn't too bad after all, the coming debate about whether ambition was a good thing or not and how Rosemary was learning Woolsey's bit about flinging it away, by that sin fell the angels, intending to bring it into her speech as if she'd thought of it that minute, or even as if she'd made it up—but she wouldn't get away with that. The flush died out of Antosia's cheeks, leaving her face milky white, with dark rings under her eyes that made them look sizes too large; but she was reviving. She was quiet now; she could listen, twirling the end of Bridget's plait that she held tight, and she could even give a grin now and then. Oh, yes, she was getting better. She was leaving the huge, tragic and incomprehensible affairs of her country and coming back to Ramparts where everyone knew where they were.

Mrs. Drake was there at the door. Bridget was reminded of the first day of all when she had arrived with Grannie. She was still the halma man with her white knob of a head and her dumpy figure that widened out with her starched apron, but though she might look the same, oh! the difference inside—and all owing to Tossie and the Blessed Bull. She was beaming at them, positively beaming.

"I thought you'd be early for your tea, so I lit the fire. The cake's come up lovely and I've an egg boiling—not having any proper breakfast nor yet any dinner, she'll need it, I said to Drake. You come in, my lambie, and take your rest—"

"Oh, Drakey, aren't you *cosy!*" cried Antosia—her favorite word. And she threw her arms round Mrs. Drake and hugged her. "Fires and hearth rugs and welcomes, all so warm—" She dropped off her coat and lay down in front of the blazing fire beside old Rouge, who thumped his tail and nuzzled his head, now grown the color of very milky coffee, into her hand. "You and I, Rouge, we're lucky—we're lucky, lucky, lucky . . . I know we are." But she buried her face in his ruff so that they shouldn't see her tears.

> 2 <

After that, life at Ramparts went on as usual, only a little faster as the Christmas holidays came in sight. Antosia's cold vanished as unaccountably as it came and no one made any comments on it, except, of course, Gossip Violet. She said, "It's a very odd sort of cold you had. You never snuffle and your nose isn't red and shiny."

"That's because I never poke it in anywhere," said Antosia seriously, as if she were describing a symptom.

"But was it an ordinary cold? Was your throat sore? Did you have a temperature? Could you talk?"

"I could talk. But if you could have heard the things I said!"

"Delirious, were you? My goodness, it must have been—"

But Bridget brought the conversation to a close. Violet was pretty slow, but she wasn't as stupid as all that.

Judy's scholarship was the next excitement.

She went up for it and was *proxime*; she might even have got it if the winner hadn't been so remarkably good at transposing, she told them. "He was marvelous, he really was. He could do anything, play things in any key, play any tunes they asked for out of his head. He had beady black eyes and long hands and I'll never be like him if I live to be a million and practice all day. Never."

"Who wants you to be like him?" said Antosia briskly.

But Judy only groaned, "I'm no good, I'm no good. I shan't try again."

Antosia took her by the shoulders and shook her.

"Never, *never* say that. You must always try again. He was a freak and a genius and he ought to be in Remove. Of course you will try again and next time he won't be there and you will get it. And you must play tunes in other keys, too. You can and you shall. Come with me now and play *Pop Goes the Weazel* in A, B, C, D, E, F and G—" And she dragged her off to a piano. Judy, like an arrow in the hands of an expert archer, was aimed at the bull's-eye all over again. (And Antosia was perfectly right; the next time there was no outstanding candidate; Judy got her scholarship and a half holiday for the rest of the form, and that was the glorious end of her as far as Ramparts was concerned.)

"My goodness, Tossie does keep us all on the hop," Bridget told Grannie at tea. "She's got us so keen on the dancing that we're going to have a Folk-dance party for break-up. The whole of the Sixth are doing the Robber Dance and in the Upper Fifth we're going all Scottish with an Eightsome and Reels and Rory O'More, and Elspeth hounding after us like a sheep dog—at least Tossie says she's like a sheep dog. She won't let Tossie do the sword dance, though. She's got it wrong—much too Polish and temperamental, Elspeth says."

"Elspeth's very strict, but I'm in the eightsome and the reels and I'm going to sing *Auld Lang Syne*," said Antosia, comfortably.

"But do you know what the words mean?" inquired Grannie.

"No. But I needn't. It means you make new friends but you keep the old—my father told me that. He always sang it whenever he could, though he never understood a word except the cup of kindness; he said that meant a cup of tea."

"*Tea?*" snorted Grannie. "A lot he knew!"

"But tea is very kind—"

"Well, anyhow the party is something to look forward to when exams are over," sighed Bridget.

Exams were ordinary school exams, but they mattered more than usual because on their results hung the decision as to who should or should not go in for the certificate in July. If you went in, you didn't act in the play, which was a pity, but on the other hand, if you passed the thing, you got into the Sixth with a lot of privileges and responsibilities and interesting new horizons ahead. Also you had a year in hand, so to speak, to spend on what you liked, and that meant a running start at whatever was your job.

"And what happens if you don't go in for it," inquired Grannie as they discussed this at supper.

"Oh, then you go into a special form next autumn and stay there till you do."

"Another sort of Remove. I should like that," said Antosia.

"I shouldn't. I'd a lot rather get into the Sixth."

"And the Captain and Head—"

"Be quiet, Tossie. Let's both go in for the Certificate."

"No. Now hearken to me and I shall prophesy." Antosia got up and struck a prophetic attitude, a bit of drapery from the piano flung across her like a toga, a fearful frown wrinkling her forehead and a startling glare in her eye. "This is my prophecy. Bridget will get thousands and thousands of marks in her exams and she will plunge into the battle for the Certificate and work like a million ants and pass it and be in the Sixth and Captain and Head Girl—"

"Bunk," put in Bridget.

"Don't interrupt. Antosia will not. She will not get thousands or even hundreds of marks, nor go into the battle, nor get into the Sixth. She will play tennis a great deal and cricket a lovely little, and she will have a heavenly long, glorious summer term and she will be very happy. *Very* happy. And she will act. She will be given the part of Rosalind—"

"Go on. *You?* Why you?"

> *"Because that I am more than common tall,*
> *That I did suit me at all points like a man—"*

"Tossie, you've been learning it."

"The cheek of you!" said Grannie. "Put that bit of embroidery back where you found it and come and finish your supper and don't talk nonsense."

"It's not nonsense, it's sense. Rosemary Parke will be Touchstone and I shall be Rosalind." Antosia ceased to prophesy and calmly took another scone.

"You don't suit at *any* point like a man, you're not in the least like one."

"I'm as like as Rosalind." Nothing shook her.

"Now don't you go giving parts round like this," said Bridget warningly, "or you'll get sat on. Addy does the casting herself. I've never seen her produce a play but the others say she's a perfect whale at it."

"I'm all the more sure then," said Antosia serenely.

"And Toinette will sing the *Hey nonny* song as Second Page—she'll never say, 'Stubbornness of fortune' so that anyone can understand her—and that girl in the Sixth who's having singing lessons will be Amiens and sing the others."

"And what about Bridget?"

"Certificate people aren't allowed to act. She'd have made a lovely Orlando—except for the plait."

The plait. The awful plait. "There, Grannie, you see what a frightful curse it is. That just shows. I'm going to have it off. I really *am*."

Antosia crowed with mysterious laughter. "No, no, don't let her. I can't do without it."

"You must ask your mother," was all Grannie would say. "Anyway, why should we believe Antosia's prophecies? I don't."

Nevertheless—as Addy would have said—half of them came true almost at once. The results of the exams, posted up at the end of term, showed Bridget's name on the list for the Certificate but not Antosia's.

"What did I tell you?" Tossie whispered. "Now you wait for the rest."

But they had to wait until the next term to hear about the play, Addy told them in her breaking-up speech. Meanwhile, would the Fifth and Sixth read it and study it and make up their minds which parts they would like to try for. She finished up Ramparts' various affairs, then she left the school and went on to talk very seriously about the war. The momentous year of 1943 was coming to an end; a still more momentous year lay ahead of them. . . . "Oh, Addy *can* talk!" Bridget said to herself as she listened to her vivid, telling phrases. "She carries us right away—" and she looked at Antosia's rapt face—"Tossie further than anyone. There she is, gone miles from Ramparts . . . I I wish she wouldn't."

It finished. Addy wished them all as merry a Christmas as possible and might the New Year bring them all the happiness of peace; and they all stood up to sing.

Rosemary Parke leaned across. "There won't be any peace in the Upper Fifth till I get the mine sweeper's parcel off," she whispered in her dry way. She was the secretary for it and a pair of gloves, a scarf and two pairs of socks were still to come. But Antosia didn't smile; she wasn't listening. She was staring at the *Reading Lady* over Addy's head, lost in it.

➤ 3 ◄

They went back to Scaurbank for the Easter holidays, to help plant potatoes. They arrived on a Friday, Maggie's market day, and there she was in her market clothes at the station to meet them, her parcels and baskets and string bags beside her, just the same as ever.

"Eh, but you've grown, you've changed!" was all she could say.

"Of course we've grown, we're nearly a year older. And Tossie's hair doesn't go flopping over her face any more."

"But you haven't, Maggie, thank goodness you haven't!" cried Antosia, as they both hugged her. "You're just exactly the same as ever. Let's run—"

"Run?—Ronnie's got the car—"

"She means are you as busy as ever."

"Me? Busier. Far busier. I've got me sitting hens, and I've forty-two young pigs and what they're going to eat, I'm sure I don't know, with no meal for them with this war—Ronnie says they've the look of greyhounds, but how can I help that? And there's two sick cows in the byre—that's the medicine for them in the beer bottles in me basket. And Ronnie had a nasty kick from the mare a while back and I've had to do the milking—but he's right again. He's outside in the car with the trailer—been selling pigs and I tell him we need to sell some more and get them out of my way—and we're all pleased to see you both, I can tell you, grown so tall and all—"

By the time they were at Scaurbank gates they were deep in it; they might never have been away. They changed into the right sort of clothes and took a walk around the yard with Ronnie, visited the sick cows and helped to administer a bottle of the medicine. Then they looked at the chickens with Maggie, the "little loves," as Antosia called them, holding their soft down against her face. And they called on the newest family of pigs.

Antosia picked one up. "Feel it, Bridget. A warmish hot water bottle filled rather too full and smelling of curry —let's take one home to Green Hedges. Oh, isn't it grand to be back. Where shall we go now, Maggie? What about that foal?"

But Maggie was gone, running as hard as ever after her work and still as far as ever from catching it up. There was nothing they could do to help until it was time to get supper, so they strolled down to the river and sat on the edge of the bank to take a long look at everything.

"Gosh, yes, it's heavenly to be back," said Bridget. "But it looks different though, doesn't it? The haycocks pretty well gone and most of the straw, the barley field ploughed up and us putting potatoes into it tomorrow. And the light's different and the sky and the air—"

Then they looked at the chickens with Maggie

"It's all entirely different," said Antosia decidedly. "There's no Krak."

No Krak. Yes, that was a huge difference, though Bridget hadn't thought of it.

Krak's name hadn't come up for a very long time. They had had a busy spring term, deep in the play, everyone soaked in it. Even Bridget, who was only allowed to understudy and never attended rehearsals if she didn't want to, knew it by heart. Antosia's prophecies had turned out perfectly correct. She had been given the part of Rosalind,

Rosemary Parke was Touchstone, and Toinette was doing the form great credit by the way she sang *When birds do sing, hey ding a ding ding, Sweet lovers love the spring*— all exactly as Tossie had said. And she was adoring it all. Never, she declared, had she been so happy in all her life. Addy told her she had a "feeling" for production and turned to her in the most flattering way with, "What do you think, Antosia?" when she wanted another opinion—or sent her to coach people with dull voices— "Put some life into her—you know what I mean."

All this was so far removed from Krak that Bridget had almost forgotten him—and she was not sorry to do so. He was wonderful and fascinating, of course, but he meant Poland to Antosia and *As You Like It* was a long way from Poland.

However, here he was, brought to mind by Scaurbank and it would be unnatural not to follow up Tossie's remark.

"D'you know where he is?"

"He must be back, I think. Oh, I *hope* he is back."

"Where from?"

"Another mission."

So he'd been on another of his trips—no wonder they'd heard nothing of him. What had he been doing this time?

"You don't think he'll come here again, do you?"

"And make me walk that wire bridge again?" Antosia laughed and groaned. "What ages and ages ago! I've never been so frightened in all my life—no, never."

"Except when you were riding the bore."

"Ah, but I had your plait to hold on to then."

"Yes, my word, you had. I can feel it now. Don't you do any more riding because you won't have it again."

"Why not?"

"It's coming off tomorrow."

"Bridget! You don't mean it!"

"I do. I've got Mum's letter—" and she read it out. " *'It used to be the thing to put your hair up when you grew up, now apparently you cut it off. Of course you must get rid of your nice plait, darling, if it really gets in your way—'* It does get in my way—it'll be dangling all over the place when we're planting potatoes, so I shall go in by bus tomorrow and find a hairdresser, and that'll be that."

Antosia seized it and gave it a sharp pull.

"That's the last time you do that, my girl."

"Can I have it?"

"Cut off, d'you mean?"

"Yes. Rosemary has a fox brush hanging on the wall, I shall have Bridget's plait."

"As long as I don't have to look at it, you can do what you like with the thing."

They were good holidays; not as exciting perhaps as the summer ones, but then, as Antosia had remarked, there was no Krak. They kept on talking of him, especially when they went down to the river, as they did most evenings.

"D'you remember the way Krak ran, simply *ran* with that sheep?"

"Yes. My goodness he was strong. And what a little idiot you were to think you could hold it for half a second."

"Hm. I nearly sprained my wrist that time."

"Did you? You never said so. And you took all the skin off your knee. Now don't you go doing silly things like that for him again, will you?"

"No, Grandmother Bridget. Not like *that*."

Something in her voice made Bridget ask sharply, "Like what then?"

But Antosia was silent, her eyes fixed on a gull that swooped about over the river, tacking up against the wind. Gosh, she's not going Polish again, is she? thought Bridget, looking at her with a sinking heart. It was extraordinary the way Tossie simply *left*, went somewhere else, when Krak's name came up. Her body stayed behind but her mind flew off like a bird out of a cage. And Scaurbank was haunted by him. Wherever they went, it didn't matter how far, he seemed to go with them.

"There's Czartorya," Tossie said one day when they were having a long walk and the blue mountains of the Lakes cut into the sky in front of them.

"Skiddaw," corrected Bridget.

"No, Czartorya. Where the thousand knights are waiting in their cave—don't you remember?"

"Oh, yes, I believe I do, you talked about them that wire bridge day—you and Krak. One looks out and says, 'Is it time?' and sighs—"

"No, *doesn't* sigh. Doesn't sigh any more—laughs—" and suddenly Antosia went dancing down the road in a way that reminded Bridget of her prancing down the boat deck, singing "Tuesday, Tuesday, Tuesday—" when her thirteenth birthday was coming. Bobby White's mother had said she moved like a young cat, and she did still.

"What does he do then?" asked Bridget when Tossie came back.

"After he has laughed, he roars. He ROARS."

"Why? Got a pain?"

"No, no, *no!* Relief, joy, triumph—victory!"

"Gosh," murmured Bridget, because she had nothing she could possibly say that would match the extraordinary tone of Tossie's voice. "Is that what Krak says?"

"What Krak will say when we see him."

And in the house it was just the same. Hardly a meal passed that one of the household didn't ask how he was, what he was doing, when he was coming back.

"Eh, but he had an arm! He could lift a cow, that uncle of yours—a biggish calf anyway."

"And run—see him turn the sheep on the marsh—good as a sheep dog."

"A grand man to have beside you—"

"Not in a boat—" Bridget managed to slip in.

"No, not in a boat," agreed Antosia, "—unless you've a hair rope to hold on to—" And no one could make out what she was laughing at.

So much did they talk of him that it hardly seemed a surprise when they got back to Green Hedges and Drakey met them on the doorstep with, "Your uncle's come." Bridget had almost expected him. When they walked in, lo! there he was, having tea with Grannie, the round table cosily between them. It was so like that first day when she had come back from Ramparts that she found herself saying, "You haven't left Tossie at the hotel this time."

Krak was quick; he understood at once.

"No. She's sure of her welcome now. But you haven't said, 'Hallo.' And where's your plait?"

"Yes, *where's* your plait?" cried Grannie, in a shocked voice.

"Here," cried Antosia and whisked it out of her pocket.

"Bridget! What frightful thing have you done!"

The plait in fact was a godsend. It gave them time to get over the surprise of finding Krak, and it started the conversation with a laugh, a good thing when it's going to

There he was, having tea with Grannie

be serious. For it was serious. Grannie said, "Well, Antosia, your uncle's come to say good-bye. Really good-bye this time, I'm afraid."

Yes, it was really good-bye. No more missions, no more training. They were off.

"Oh, where, Krak?" breathed Antosia.

"Out of Scotland anyway."

"'The shortest way to Poland'?"

"Hope so," said Krak, and smiled at her. But it wasn't the old grin. Krak had altered; looking at him, Bridget couldn't make up her mind how. He was older of course—perhaps it was that. His face was brown, but not bronzed as it had been that time he had walked into the Scaurbank

scullery and found her washing up. He didn't look like a
magnificent bronze statue come to life any more. He was
very lean, not to say thin, his face had hollows under the
cheekbones, and he had a five-barred gate on his forehead
that never used to be there.

"You've been ill, haven't you?" said Bridget.

"No, not ill. I was a little stupid, did not take enough
care, when I was away."

"How long have you been back?" asked Antosia anxiously.

"Not long."

"Was it when you were on your mission that you were—
stupid?"

"Yes." Krak gave her almost his old grin. "But only for
three days. Bad days, though."

"Oh, Krak—"

What were they talking about, these two? You never
knew. Bridget frowned and wished she had read the papers
as assiduously as Antosia—she always had from the beginning. Now she read Grannie's weeklies, beside *The Times*,
and there wasn't a word in one of them even remotely
connected with Poland that she hadn't devoured. What
had been happening? Krak had been "underground" again,
had he? And what was the "carelessness" that had changed
him like this? She wasn't to know. The conversation, whatever it was about, was short. Krak had only come for an
hour or so, to say good-bye. He must go, he said, and he'd
take Antosia to the station to see him off— "I've plenty
to tell her." His taxi, in fact, was at the door even now.
He said his good-byes—and very beautifully and gratefully
did he say them—and off they went.

Feeling extraordinarily flat, Bridget sat down to finish her tea.

"That uncle of Antosia's brought some news today," said Grannie.

"Did he? I wish he'd talk more about what he does—I'm sure it's so exciting. But he never does except to Tossie—blow all the Security! What was it?"

"Antosia's father is on his way to England."

"Her *father?*" Bridget put down her cup in amazement. "But it's years—"

"Yes, years. Years since she heard from him."

"She's never had a letter since she's been here."

"No. He went back to Poland, apparently, and was caught. They didn't kill him, though, and he escaped and did a lot of marvelous work in Warsaw. Then he was caught again and a couple of months ago they rescued him —I think Krak did that. Anyway, they caught Krak and held him for three days and he had to be rescued, too. I gather he had an appalling time. No wonder he looks like that—you noticed it, I saw. The things they do, these men, dropping each other about out of aeroplanes like parcels —oh, the appalling things that happen in Poland! We're never half thankful enough that we live on our island, our blessed plot, and not there—"

"Tossie wouldn't live anywhere else for the world."

"No, of course she wouldn't. Still, let's be thankful for the luck of England in being just where it is. Well, as I was saying, they rescued her father and now he's been given a very important job and he's coming to London."

"What? To live?"

"No. To see them all and be off again—at least that's what the uncle thinks."

"Tossie doesn't know all this, does she?"

"I don't see how she could. He hasn't been able to write."

"All the same I believe she guesses. She's been happier about things lately."

Bridget had a vision of Antosia dancing down the road crying, "He doesn't sigh any more—he laughs—he *roars!*" when they were talking about the knight who looked out of his cave and asked, "Is it time?"

"Did Krak say when he was coming?" Bridget asked.

"No. Soon, he seemed to think."

Soon. Bridget relapsed into silence and in an absent-minded way went on with her tea. Soon. Antosia's father might be coming soon. What would he be like? Daddy had said he was fascinating and that he told a very good story—not much help. What would he want her to do? He wouldn't surely take Tossie away—oh, he *couldn't!* . . . something in Bridget reared up like a frightened horse at the very idea. He surely couldn't, just when she had Rosalind to act and the singles for Ramparts to play and all the summer term, what she called the heavenly-long summer term, stretching before her. Surely, surely not.

➤ 4 ＜

Looking back on that summer term long after it was over, Bridget saw it as a race; not her race against time but time's race against Tossie's father.

When Antosia came back that day from the station after seeing Krak off, they sat over the fire, the three of them, and talked. Antosia talked more freely than Bridget had ever heard her, about her country and herself. For one thing, Krak had told her that she might, and for another, she now felt she could.

"I couldn't before," she said. "Even if it hadn't been Security I couldn't, because when I talked my courage went down and down till it ran away out of my toes. It's easier to have courage when you're silent."

"Is it?" asked Grannie, interested in this. "I'm not so sure."

"For me it is. After I had read the papers that made me cry, I used to look at Bridget doing sums and think of Ramparts and the *Reading Lady* and then I felt better. Wait, I used to say to myself, and be calm and busy like that. Besides, Krak told me I must learn to keep Polish things to myself and not bother the English with them too much. And never to worry. But I did worry. I was always afraid for him whenever he went on his missions— I always shall be. I think he will be forever running into every kind of danger because he is like that. But my father is different. I always felt in my bones that he was alive somewhere. He is very clever and experienced and he would be very, very careful because he knows he must live to work for Poland. He never wrote but still I felt sure."

"Well, you were quite right," said Grannie. "The prophet once more."

Antosia laughed at that. But when Bridget suggested that she should drape the piano cover over her shoulders and stand up and give them some more prophecies, this time about what her father was likely to do with her when he came, her face clouded over. She clapped both hands to her head, as she always did when she was worrying over a sum that wouldn't come out, and said, "You have a proverb that says don't cross your bridges till you come to them—we haven't come to that bridge."

"A very sensible remark," said Grannie. "Possibly it won't have to be crossed. Now let's wash up." And there the conversation ended.

They didn't mention the father's coming, or Krak, or anything to do with Poland again. It was a sort of tacit agreement between them that, since they hadn't come to the bridge, it should be forgotten until they did. Antosia took a header into Ramparts and its many affairs and seemed altogether swallowed up by it. You wouldn't have thought she had an idea beyond school and work and games and her acting.

"I'm going to have the fullest, the very cram-fullest term anyone has ever had," she cried, as they rode along to their first morning. It was one of those emerald and gold May mornings that are full of not only the sight but the sound of spring; when you seem to hear the leaves hurrying out on the trees and the crack of the eggs as the nestlings burst forth; a morning when the warm earth leaps forward towards June and high summer with every instrument in its whole glorious orchestra playing its music.

"Hey, ding-a-ding-a-ding," Tossie carolled, and she might have been one of the bird chorus herself, swooping along, hands waving nowhere near the handle bars, head thrown back. "This is the Forest of Arden—we're in it now and Rosalind's got a bicycle, of course she has. Why doesn't she sing in the play? She'd be singing half the time."

"Put a song in for her," suggested Bridget. "Addy says you have a feeling for production and perhaps poor old Shakespeare hadn't."

"Sarcastic old cat, aren't you—oh, there's Elspeth—"

And not only Elspeth but most of the form. They had turned out in a body to meet them. There was a lot going on already and in a moment they were caught up in it. Bridget and Antosia were the tennis pair for the form and the draw for the tournament was up on the board. They had to play the Sixth.

"What? First go off? How simply awful," cried Bridget, appalled.

But Antosia didn't think it awful. She set to work at once, arranging practice matches—there was a fortnight to go, heaps of time, but balls were scarcer than ever and you had to be fair with them. Bicycles were shoved away, shoes changed, and they moved over to Hall in a body, exchanging news as they went. Form cricket captains were to be voted for in break. Of course Bridget was going to be elected again, she'd done very well for them last year, but a bit of canvassing was going on.

Miss Sharp of the Upper Fourth had left, gone nursing, and a funny old bird with an Eton crop had come instead. Addy had a new gray suit; she'd spoken at a headmistress' conference or something frightfully grand like that in it. Rosemary Parke's sister had heard her and said she was marvelous; one of the people there had said she ought to stand for Parliament. Well, why shouldn't she? It would be a leg-up for Ramparts. The Games Mistress had sworn to play a single with every tennis player in the Fifth and Sixth before she made out the handicaps for the American tournament—she was a fair old thing. They were starting Guide Cadets. The sixteens had to register. The Wrens had a waiting list miles long—the thing to go for now was the Fannies . . . and then they were in Hall, quiet now, with the *Reading Lady* taking no notice whatever of them, not even when Addy came in and stood in front of her, hiding her little satin shoes. The wheel of Ramparts was once again turning and they were all happily turning with it, Bridget and Antosia closer and closer to the hub.

> 5 <

If Antosia wanted a cram-full term, she was certainly getting it. Tennis became of enormous importance. Once again she was up early, hitting her one precious ball against her wall, getting her eye in; and, what was more, she had Bridget up, too.

"Of course you must get into the Six—it'll do your Certificate good, so don't say you haven't time. Right foot across—no, *right* foot across for the backhands—turn sideways to the wall. Quick—run in and volley—" Tossie made Bridget work at it as she never had before. "If you get into the Six, we go to matches together and that's much more fun. Let's do everything together we possibly can this term. I'll never get into the Eleven, but you can get into the Six and you must."

Antosia herself was very soon chosen for the singles. "Didn't I say so the very first time I saw her?" said the Games Mistress proudly, and went off to ring up the Waafs at the Unit to arrange a match.

"We're pretty strong this year," they said doubtfully.

"So are we," said Miss Harrison.

"We've got a girl who nearly won the schools championship at Wimbledon. We'd better send you our second string."

"No, don't. We'll give you a game, don't you worry," said the Games Mistress, and fixed a date at the end of

June when *As You Like It* and all the excitements of half term would be over. Antosia, if Miss Harrison was not very much mistaken, was of the stuff of which Wimbledon was made and she was not in the least afraid. But she must learn to place her serve; it was fast, but pace isn't enough. Miss Harrison rang off and sought Antosia out for half an hour's practice.

And the play. The play, Antosia said, was pure heaven. now that Addy took most of the rehearsals.

"But need Antosia spend quite all this time on the understudies?" asked Grannie, a little mystified, when Tossie had left her half-finished tea and flown back to Ramparts for the third time that week. "You're a very healthy lot of girls; it's most unlikely that they'll be wanted. And you're one, Bridget, and you don't seem to rehearse much."

"It's Elspeth mostly. She's understudying Rosalind and Tossie's helping her. I'm understudying Touchstone."

"She doesn't bother much with you."

"No."

And why? Bridget knew as well as she knew her own name. Antosia was getting Rosemary ready in case something happened, in case she had to go. Ramparts mustn't on any account be let down. And that was why she had tried so hard to get the Unit match put earlier. The school second string wasn't up to much and Miss Harrison had set her heart on winning that match. Tossie wasn't saying any of this, of course. The bridge hadn't to be crossed yet; on the contrary it seemed further off. It was June now; the play was in a fortnight and nothing had been heard of her father. If he was on a ship, surely he'd have sent a radio message—but traveling had changed, you never knew nowadays where people were or how fast they were going; they reached England in all sorts of complicated ways. Still, here they were practically in June— Then Bridget took herself to task. Don't be too cocksure, she said to herself severely; he *may* come and he *may* carry Antosia away. In theory she believed in facing things, in looking them squarely in the face; but in practice she always followed up the horrible idea with a consoling, "But he won't, of course he won't." For it was truly a horrible idea. Ramparts without Tossie . . .

She couldn't help feeling more and more cheerful as the first week of lovely June ran away in a delicious stream of days and hours; work, cricket, more work, tennis; playing in the Six, watching Tossie win her first singles 6.2, 6.2, and the next 6.1, 6.1; prompting her in that scene with Orlando when she was the "saucy lackey," making fun of him. They did manage to do a lot of things together, in spite of their different work and their different games.

"Let's dash back and have tea with Grannie," suggested Bridget one specially busy afternoon. "We've got the Lower Fifth to play but not till six (they had won their victory over the Sixth after taking each set to ten all—what a game that had been!) I've booked a court. I'll do my homework after supper."

"All right, let's. I've got a rehearsal with Addy at quarter to seven in the garden. We don't come in fast enough, she says, we've got to start earlier, or nearly run or something. It's no joke getting it all ready for either out of doors or Hall. I do think your weather might make up its mind—"

"Now you hush up about the weather. You've had three years of it nearly—don't pretend you're not used to it."

They rode back together. There were no cars about these

days and they went along side by side, talking hard, even when they had to push their bicycles up the last bit of the hill. At the top, the place where Antosia had caught that first glimpse of Drakey's Bull, they always started a race for home, with a strict rule that you coasted until a certain tree was passed. Bridget had her foot on the pedal and was shouting, "Are you ready? One—two, three—" when Antosia said, "Look, there's a car at Green Hedges."

"Grannie being fetched away to that old canteen. I bet Mrs. Abel's ratted again—"

"It's too big for that," said Antosia in a queer breathless voice, and shot away, pedaling hard.

Bridget followed; but slowly, her brake on. She wanted time to collect herself, to breathe evenly, to get ready. The car, when she came to look at it, was long and slim. It was khaki, with dark blobs and streaks of camouflage; not the sort of car they ever had at Green Hedges. It was—yes, she was perfectly certain it was—Antosia's father.

She took both bicycles around to the side of the house.

"Who is it, Drakey?" she asked at the back door. But of course she knew without waiting for the answer—

"It's him. There's a girl chauffeur. Polish. She'll be wanting her tea—where'll she—"

Then Grannie came into the kitchen.

"Oh, Bridget, darling, I rang you up at school but they said you'd started. I've left them together—three years since she's seen him. It's a lifetime at Antosia's age—" She was excited, moved, perturbed as Bridget had never seen her.

"What's he like?" Bridget asked, staving off the moment when she knew she must ask the real question—what's he going to do with Tossie?

"Oh, he's wonderful of course, after all he's been through. He's rather—terrific. Antosia's eyes, a huge forehead with gray hair standing up above it. I see where she gets her vitality. And I see what your father meant. Yes, he is fascinating—in a way. But, oh, poor Poland—" She was almost incoherent, trying to break to Bridget the news she had to give. "I'm afraid he wants Antosia. I'm afraid he's going to take her away—he's full of all sorts of schemes and plans—and she's nearly sixteen, you know. It seems young to us but it doesn't to him. The Polish girls and boys, they're a miracle—they do the most amazing, unheard of things—"

Bridget gulped, and got out a word— "When?"

"I'm afraid—now."

"Oh." The kitchen table was handy to perch on just till this roaring in her ears stopped. Why it should make one go all dizzy to hear something said that one always knew would be said—

"He can't go doing that," said Mrs. Drake belligerently and crashed down the tea tray on the dresser.

"Yes, he can. I'm afraid he must. Oh, Bridget, I'm so sorry—"

And then Bridget heard Tossie's voice calling her and she ran.

➤ 6 ◄

Perhaps, she thought afterwards, it was a good thing that it had all to be done in such a hurry. Antosia's departure had all the flurry and excitement and whirlwind feeling of an accident and there was no time to think or talk too much. Her father went off to Ramparts to see Addy, and Grannie went with him to show the way.

Drakey was humming and buzzing around her kitchen like a furious bee, cutting sandwiches, making Antosia her favorite little cakes to take with her, filling their thermos with coffee. They had to be back in London that night, there was no time even for tea. He'd no business to be doing this, father or not, she said, and flicked off an angry tear with her oven cloth. Packing had to be done as fast as possible.

"We'll do it together, Bridget. I'll get the things and you put them in. And I'll talk the whole time because if I don't, I shall cry," said Antosia. "My things are all to go to Madame Someone in London and tomorrow she's to take me out for two hours' shopping when I buy all the things I must. And then at twelve o'clock we go."

"In a boat—you'll enjoy that," said Bridget, trying to grin.

"No, not a boat, an aeroplane. But I shall take my blanket. Leave it out, the darling thing, and I'll carry it as I always do. It's because places are so hard to get that I must fly off like this. They brought my father back on a destroyer. He's got permission to take me—"

"Where?"

"I'm not sure. To Russia, I think, and then—home."

"Poland, you mean?" Right up there? Bridget's heart turned to lead.

"Yes. My father thinks we shall be home by Christmas."

"But what are you going to do? Not—not go 'underground'—"

"I don't know—perhaps that'll be over. He says it's the future we must work for now. We must forget the past and start again—"

"Like Addy and her history—"

"Yes, just like. They want people who are young and people who can speak English, he says. I am to train—"

Bridget burst out, "But not *yet*. Must you go *now*? Can't you wait till August anyway? Why must you fly off like this? We've got a form match at six." She burst into shaky laughter to think of it. "Oh, Tossie, I can't stand it —you can't go—"

Antosia sat down on the bed beside her.

"Oh, Bridget, how awful it is! I was always afraid it would be like this."

"So was I."

"I know—but what was the good of talking about it. We've had a lovely term—half of it. Now here's the bridge to be crossed."

"And it's a foul wire bridge."

"Foul," agreed Antosia. "And Krak and all my relations on the other side. So you see I must go. I *must*." Then she jumped up and put her head out of the window, just as she had that night at Scaurbank. When she came back her voice was lighter again. "I shall howl like a wolf for you when I've gone—just put my head back and *howl*—for you and for Ramparts, and my lovely Rosalind and that Unit tennis match, and for Addy standing up there in front of the *Reading Lady*, saying all her things—but most of all, far most of all, for you. But now, listen, Bridget—we'll talk for two minutes and then we'll go on packing. I'll be the grandmother this time. Listen, you must come to Poland— soon, quite soon. My father says lots of you English came after the last war and helped to make the country again. They're getting themselves trained now. Haven't you seen about them and all the training they're doing in the papers? You get your old Certificate and a bit of their training and then come, too. Will you?"

Bridget nodded. It was an idea, anyway.

"That's a date then—I'll book a court—" Then she half laughed, half moaned, "Oh, you will apologize to Miss Harrison for me, won't you. She'll never forgive me. Tell them all what you like—Violet will worm it out of you anyhow. Addy'll understand, she'll have seen father. Tell Miss Harrison I'll be back one day to play at her old Wimbledon she thinks such a lot of. And tell Elspeth she's got to play *up* and then she'll be a grand Rosalind. Now we'd better get on with this blessed packing. Let's get Rouge and James to help."

Old Rouge with his charming way of prowling about, tail wagging and a pair of shoes in his soft, rubbery mouth, and James, who always knew when something was up, yapping around him, certainly made it easier. They packed as hard as they knew how; the last of the suitcases was hauled down the stairs as the car drove up.

"No good-byes—we won't say them," whispered Antosia. "It's *dowidzenia*—that's the Polish for *au revoir*, till I see you again. Say it."

"*Dowidzenia*," said Bridget.

"Bridget's coming to stay with us as soon as the war's over," cried Antosia airily, as she introduced her father. He bent over Bridget's hand and said he was delighted to hear it. Yes, he was like Tossie, the same warm, interested look in his eye, the same lively way of speaking.

"Now we must say our last thank yous, our last good-byes. Are you ready, Antosia?"

"Yes, Father. Oh, where's my blanket—"

"Here you are, Tossie."

Good-bye, good-bye—the car slid away. *What* was it

Tossie was waving out of the window? Could it be—yes, it was . . . a plait of hair tied with a Ramparts ribbon.

Bridget felt in her pocket for the half-sixpence the Second Officer had provided; they'd changed halves again, slipping them into each other's hands under the blanket. I must remember that Polish word, she said to herself. Good-bye till I see you again.